# The Merchant Bank Mystery

John Waddington-Feather

Copyright © 2015 John Waddington-Feather

All rights reserved.

The characters and events in this book are fictitious. Any similarity to real persons, living or dead, is co-incidental and not intentional.

No part of this book may be reproduced, stored in a retrieval system or transmitted in any form or by any means without express permission of the publisher.

Feather Books SY3 0BW UK

**ISBN-13:**
978-1515155591

**ISBN-10:**
1515155595

## PROFILE

John Waddington-Feather is an Anglican NSM priest. He has written children's books (one of which was nominated for the Carnegie Medal in 1989) and his verse-play Garlic Lane was awarded the Burton Prize in 1999. He has also written collections of verse and hymns and used to edit the Christian poetry magazine, The Poetry Church. He was a teacher for many years and also ministered in Shrewsbury Prison as a prison visitor and NSM.

# CONTENTS

| | |
|---|---|
| Chapter One | 1 |
| Chapter Two | 8 |
| Chapter Three | 15 |
| Chapter Four | 25 |
| Chapter Five | 33 |
| Chapter Six | 40 |
| Chapter Seven | 45 |
| Chapter Eight | 51 |
| Chapter Nine | 58 |
| Chapter Ten | 65 |
| Chapter Eleven | 71 |
| Chapter Twelve | 77 |
| Chapter Thirteen | 83 |
| Chapter Fourteen | 88 |

Feather Books apologise for any typos which may have been overlooked, however, phrases such as 't'olden days' or 't'church' are intentional and written to reflect the Yorkshire accent of the character concerned.

## CHAPTER ONE

There was an air of anticipation in Keighworth police station, and a good deal of apprehension. The old superintendent for the past fifteen years, Frank Balsh, had retired and a new one had been appointed: the youngest in England and a very ambitious young man.

Superintendent Frank Balsh had been well respected by everyone. Though strict, he was understanding: tempering discipline with tolerance and common sense. Like many of his generation, he'd been in the forces and seen action in the infantry during World War II, in Normandy and in the subsequent advance across Europe.

He joined the police force on demob and became a copper on the beat, before steadily working his way up to the rank of superintendent in Keighworth. He was an experienced leader and those under him had learned much from him. When the time came for him to retire, the station was a happy and contented place. He was highly thought of by those who worked there.

But now it was time for a change and the station awaited its new head, Superintendent Arthur Reginald Timothy Cholmondeley Donaldson, whose father was a retired bishop. When he arrived they were all in for a shock and his arrival caused as much upset as if a hurricane had hit the place.

The police station was in the middle of town, across the road from Town Hall Square, an open space in the centre of Keighworth, surrounded by the Carnegie Library, the Mechanics Institute, a ladies lavatory and a line of buildings which included the Masonic Hall. In the middle of the square was the war memorial with two statues: an infantryman in full kit with rifle and bayonet, and a sailor looking through his telescope straight into the ladies lavatory.

The superintendent's office looked directly down into the square and across to the Masonic Hall, where Donaldson was to become a frequent visitor in the future. Indeed, it was to be his second home.

He'd been introduced to Inspector Blake Hartley immediately after his appointment, when he was being shown round the place. Hartley was a little over six feet tall and Donaldson had to look up to him from his something around five feet nine. Donaldson had expensive sartorial tastes, unlike the inspector who was rather shabby and wore an old raincoat and trilby over a suit which had seen better days. He said that as a detective he blended in better with the crowd that way. Meeting him for the first time you wouldn't have known he was also a non-stipendiary Anglican priest. He wore no clerical collar – nor did he thrust his religion down your throat.

Hartley was a dyed-in-the-wool provincial, utterly content and happy to be living in the town where he'd grown up. By contrast, the whole focus of Donaldson's life was the South and the Home Counties around London, where he hoped to return soon as chief superintendent, after he'd done his stint in Keighworth.

Shortly after his arrival, Superintendent Arthur Donaldson let it be known he was going overhaul the station, a new broom sweeping it clean. There was nothing subtle or tactful about Donaldson despite his expensive education and upbringing. "A fresh start," he announced to the assembled staff on his first day. "New ideas, new approaches which I hope you'll all take on board. I want Keighworth police station to be the most efficient in the county; a jewel in the Chief Constable's crown."

He paused to see the effect his words were having, but was met by rows of dour northern faces, the most dour of which was Inspector Hartley's. By the time his new boss had finished speaking, Hartley had summed him up completely. He realised they had an ambitious twit on their hands and that life was going to be very different from that under his old boss.

As senior detective officer, Inspector Blake Hartley was the first to be interviewed individually by his boss. The inspector was somewhat taken aback by the transformation of the superintendent's office. Donaldson had transformed it to reflect his personal glory. A rowing oar, with the blade painted light blue and the names of the college crew on it, hung prominently on view immediately behind his desk. It hit you in the eye as you entered the room.

The next thing you noticed was a glass cabinet filled with silver cups which he'd won golfing at college and elsewhere. He'd graduated at Cambridge, but to his lasting regret had never won a Blue. It rankled that Hartley's colleague, Detective Sergeant Ibrahim Khan, an Oxford graduate, had won a golfing Blue and was captain of the Keighworth golf club team.

The mindset of the man was also mirrored in the neatness of his desk. Everything on it was laid out with precision and never varied: a masonic paperweight, a blotting pad, an ebony ruler and a notepad – nothing else. Quite different from Hartley's untidy desk, where his case notes mingled with the outline of his next sermon.

Although the superintendent was pleased with his promotion, other aspects of his new appointment didn't go down at all well: the town itself for starters. Keighworth was a typical Yorkshire industrial town spawned during the nineteenth century. The hills and moors around it held their own wild beauty, but the town itself was grey and smoky; quite different from the couth, balmy South where Donaldson had lived all his life. In Keighworth, set in the Pennine hills, it rained often, making the place look grimmer and greyer than ever.

In fact, the Donaldsons never settled in Keighworth. They rented a house in the posh suburb of Utworth for a while, then after a few months upped sticks and bought an expensive house in Ilkesworth, the spa town over the moors from Keighworth in the next valley. Ilkesworth was a more refined place altogether, a place to which the richer gentry retired: as close a resemblance to the South as anywhere else in West Yorkshire. After a year or two there, Arthur Donaldson began applying for posts back in the South and the Home Counties – but he'd a long wait in store for him.

He was very inexperienced in criminal investigation. He'd never been on the beat and had gone straight into an admin job from the police college, which he'd entered direct from university. Unlike older policemen he'd been too young to do National Service, which was a great social mixer. By contrast, Hartley had done a two-year stint in the army before joining the force and plodding the pavement in a tough part of London.

A lot of Donaldson's early training had been behind the wheel of a panda car, patrolling a residential suburb for a few months before he'd gone back indoors, planning traffic control or attending courses on office admin. In fact, much of his time had been spent doing course work at police college. Yet here he was, the youngest superintendent in England, determined to make Keighworth police station tick like the clock on his office wall.

So he was at a loss when, in the second week of his appointment, a woman was found hanging from the banister of her home, Fairfield House in Utworth, a mansion built by a wealthy mill-magnate in the nineteenth century. It stood in its own grounds at the end of a long drive. Large, expensive, wrought-iron gates, with the name of the house on them, told visitors they were entering the domain of the rich. Wealth was vaunted everywhere in the immaculately kept grounds, with their gardens, lawns and fountains. And the frontage of the house stood a monument to the master-masons and craftsmen who'd built it.

Inside, the house was lavishly furnished. Antique furniture and expensive oil paintings embellished every room. A long, winding staircase led to the bedchambers above. But it was from this staircase that hung the body of Lucinda Wilkins, the wife of the merchant banker, Robin Wilkins, who owned the house.

The daily help had found her when she reported for duty. She phoned the police and threw Donaldson into a panic. Suicide and homicide were off his radar. So he immediately sent Inspector Hartley and Sergeant Khan to investigate before he put in an appearance later.

"Mrs Wilkins usually came to the door when I rang the bell, but today she didn't and I had to let myself in," said a tearful Elsie Smith, the daily help. "The door was unlocked an' there she were – dead! Hanging from the banister! I'd a right shock, I can tell you." She burst into tears again and blew her nose loudly into her handkerchief.

Inspector Hartley told her to make herself a cup of tea in the kitchen while he and Khan examined the body. Corpses weren't Ibrahim Khan's scene at all. He was downright squeamish about dead bodies, but at least there was no gory mess with this one.

"Suicide, sir?" he suggested.

Hartley pursed his lips and looked up at the high banister, then back to the dangling corpse which hung at the end of a long rope. He glanced at her feet. "I can't believe she jumped from the landing up there, tied to the banister. If she's committed suicide she'd be more likely to stand on a chair down here and jump off it – especially if she hadn't a head for heights," he added dryly. "It's a long drop from the landing with a rope round your neck. Falling that far would damn near have pulled her head off."

His sergeant winced. "You think she's been murdered then, sir?" he asked.

"Can't say for sure till our pathologist has examined the body. He'll be here soon," said Hartley.

And when Dr Dunwell arrived he confirmed Hartley's surmise as he looked over the corpse which had been taken down. "Whoever's done this has made a professional job of it," he muttered bending over the body. "It certainly isn't suicide. See those marks on her neck?" he said, turning the head for the detectives to see.

Hartley knelt down to have a closer look, but Khan remained standing and gazed into the middle distance.

"She was gripped by gloved hands and strangled," continued Dunwell. "Then she was strung up from the banister to make it look like suicide. Only it wasn't. It was homicide. Any idea who might have done it, Blake? Where's her husband?"

"It can't have been him. He's been in London all week. He's a merchant banker and has an apartment in the City. I've checked him out," said Hartley. "He's on his way back now."

Later, Robin Wilkins arrived home. He was of medium height and in good shape because he exercised daily in a gym. He was impeccably dressed and no doubt patronised a Savile Row tailor. As the two detectives got to know him better, they discovered he was a ladies' man and had an attractive mistress who worked as his PA. He was very smooth-tongued and Superintendent Donaldson and his wife Daphne were taken in by him at once when they met him at a Masonic Lodge open night.

When her boss arrived, Elsie Smith re-joined the detectives and Robin Wilkins, and with much eye-dabbing and nose-blowing repeated in detail just how she'd found Mrs Wilkins hanging in the hall.

Wilkins listened calmly, showing no emotion, which surprised the others. He looked sad enough but all he said was, "I suspect she was in one of her bouts of the depression she was being treated for. She often had long periods of depression. I tried to persuade her to come to live in

London with me but London wasn't her scene. She was very much a Keighworth woman. All her friends and family were here. But what on earth drove her to suicide? Her depression had never been that bad before."

"Would you like a cup o' tea, sir?" asked kindly Elsie Smith.

"That's very kind of you, Elsie," Wilkins replied. "It's been a tiring drive from London." He strolled to the lounge windows just in time to see Donaldson drive up. He displayed no grief to him either when the superintendent commiserated with him, but Donaldson commented later to Hartley that that was the way Wilkins and his sort were brought up – stiff upper lip and all that.

However, Wilkins did react when Hartley said that Mrs Wilkins' death might not have been suicide and that he was keeping an open mind about it.

"What reason have you to believe it wasn't suicide, inspector?" he asked quickly, looking hard at Hartley, who remained his usual dour, impassive self. Wilkins read nothing there.

"I wouldn't like to say, sir, till our investigations are complete," was all he offered. But his rather curt reply was sufficient for Wilkins to complain to Donaldson the next day when he met him at the Masonic Hall.

## CHAPTER TWO

Superintendent Donaldson was keen to cement his new friendship with Robin Wilkins. He always did his homework on the big names he met, and when he found out Wilkins was a wealthy merchant banker in London, who spent most of the week in the City, he was on to him in a flash - another name to add to his list.

He made a point of meeting up with Wilkins again the next day at the Lodge. He began by offering his condolences about Mrs Wilkins, but was brought up short when the other complained about Hartley's reluctance to give him more information after he'd hinted that Lucinda Wilkins had not committed suicide.

"Oh, that's just my inspector carrying out routine procedure. He's a stickler for that," said Donaldson weakly, for to tell the truth he was rather caught off guard. Hartley, he was to discover, had a habit of dropping him in it. He continued with, "I'm afraid my inspector has been over-cautious. I'll look over his report when I get back to the office. I expect it's just routine procedure."

Wilkins thanked him and looked relieved. He'd weighed up Donaldson and knew where he stood with him, but Hartley was a different matter. However, Donaldson was surprised to learn that Wilkins had been married twice, in both cases to very rich widows and both had died suddenly at Utworth.

His first wife was discovered dead in the swimming pool in their home, and now his second wife had apparently hanged herself there. When Hartley pointed this out to his boss, Donaldson shrugged it off as a coincidence. The husband couldn't have been involved in any way because he was working away in London when they died.

"You're not suggesting Mr Wilkins was in some way responsible, I hope, Hartley," he said.

Hartley replied quietly, "I'm not suggesting anything, sir, just yet. I'm simply pointing out the factual data you keep mentioning."

Donaldson knew that Hartley was getting at him, for the superintendent was always banging on about his officers collecting 'factual data' and not relying on guesswork or intuition. Donaldson was a great one for using any new jargon he picked up on the courses he frequently attended.

Moreover, once he'd added someone to his name-dropping list, it remained there unless the owner did something drastic to have it removed. But most names remained and grew in stature as time went by.

Yet there were occasions when names were dropped on account of Hartley's dogged investigations; and once dropped, those names were never referred to again. As time went by, Donaldson was very wary of Hartley and sometimes put the brakes on his inspector's investigations, till Hartley cottoned on and simply by-passed his boss.

During a routine meeting with Hartley, he brought up the subject of Mrs Wilkins' death. "Why do you believe it wasn't suicide, Hartley?" he began. "It seems pretty straightforward to me. But what you said in your report obliged the coroner to leave an open verdict, and that upset Mr Wilkins greatly."

"I'm sorry about that, sir, but the evidence all points to homicide in my opinion. Did you notice the length of the rope and the height she was supposed to have fallen?" said Hartley.

Donaldson paused for a moment, then said thoughtfully, "Yes, I did think the rope was unusually long."

"So long that the fall would have pulled her head from her body," said Hartley bluntly, making his boss wince.

Donaldson quickly changed the subject and discussed other routine matters like beat allocation, office routine and area-watch committee meetings, so that Hartley was glad to leave and get back to some honest sleuthing.

He'd been at the Railway Tavern the previous week after a choir practice at church, when a friend, Jack Lawson, had approached him about a suspected painting fraud and asked if he could speak privately with him. They adjourned to a side-room where Jack told him all.

Jack owned a small art gallery where he displayed and sold local artists' work as well as art accessories. He seemed very concerned about some paintings by the old art master at the grammar school someone had brought into his shop.

"You'll have heard that our old art master, Harry Harper, hit the headlines recently," he began.

"Yes. I read all about him in the local press," Hartley replied. "It said his work had become very famous in America, and I'm not surprised. He was a talented artist – and a great teacher. I learned a lot about life from him as well as art."

"Exactly," continued Jack Lawson. "As you know, he was very religious and left teaching late on in life to become a Catholic priest before he finally retired to Assisi as a chaplain to the cathedral there."

"So I gather," said Hartley.

"And while he was there, his paintings attracted many American admirers. In fact, his work became so popular he was invited to go on a lecture tour in the States. Some of his paintings fetch over £100,000 at auction now."

"Never!" exclaimed Hartley. "I've got one he gave me years ago when I got married; and I know of several other folk round Keighworth he gave his paintings to while he lived here."

"And that's causing a problem," said Lawson, looking worried.. "Since they've soared in price, someone's started forging them and selling them on the open market as originals."

"Any idea who?" asked Hartley.

"Somebody local I think. Somebody who's a superb painter and who is familiar with Harry Harper's style and his paintings of the area round here. Only an expert could tell the difference between the forgeries and the real thing."

"Someone like yourself?" suggested Hartley. "You're the art expert in Keighworth."

"The town has a reputation for producing good artists, surrounded by moors and the Yorkshire Dales; not to mention its industrial heritage. It's settings like this which inspired Lowry and other northern artists," said Lawson before returning to his group in the pub.

Hartley said he'd investigate, but he hadn't realised just how valuable his old art master's work had become. He said he'd visit Jack Lawson's studio the following day when the art dealer would show him the forgery.

Next day was bright and sunny as he left the police station. He loved strolling through the town, rain or shine, chatting with the odd friend or acquaintance, subconsciously checking everything out both as policeman and priest; and on his way to the studio he called in at a newsagent's to buy the morning paper. The shop was owned by an old friend, Freddy Greenwood.

"Morning, Freddy. How's things?" he began.

"Middling - but It's sad about Mrs Wilkins of Fairfield House, isn't it?" he said as he handed Blake Hartley his paper.

"You knew her?" he asked.

"She bought her paper here," said the newsagent, then leaned across the counter and lowered his voice. "A rum business the deaths of both wives, don't you think? I suppose you know old Wilkins kept a string of fancy women in London?"

Hartley was all ears at once. "No. I didn't know," he said.

Freddy said he'd found out quite by chance. His cousin was a taxi driver in the City and was hired regularly by Robin Wilkins, currently living with a young woman who acted as his PA, he said.

"The old story," said Hartley, pocketing his newspaper. "Anyhow, thanks for the info, Freddy. I'll bear it in mind."

It was titbits of gossip like this which Inspector Hartley found useful in his job, for they often filled in gaps in his investigations. If Wilkins was playing fast and loose in London and wanted rid of his wife, he could quite easily have hired a professional killer to get rid of her.

But as the inspector strolled across the road to Jack Lawson's studio his mind was on forged paintings. Lawson's Art Gallery had been there as long as he could remember for Jack Lawson took it over from his father. Hartley had frequented it often as a boy to buy his paints and paper. And now his wife, Mary, went there to buy her brushes and paints for she was a keen artist.

The shop had a large double-fronted window and stood in a row of shops. Next door was a draper's shop and the other side a shoe shop.

On display were all the necessities used in art: brushes, paints, easels and a couple of small paintings by a local artist. More of these were displayed inside on the walls and all for sale. Not for sale and in pride of place was a Lowry, which Jack's father had purchased years before.

Beneath it hung three of Harry Harper's paintings; two were of local scenes but the third had a religious motif. Blake Hartley recognised it at once for it had hung in the top corridor of his old grammar school. It had been painted by Harry Harper in memory of the old boys killed during the war, his former pupils.

It depicted the risen Christ coming out of Gordale Scar, a well-known landmark in the Dales. When the grammar school became comprehensive, the painting had been thrown out along with the old school photographs going back to the year dot. Somehow, they'd found their way into second-hand dealers' shops but had been rescued from there by Jack Lawson who displayed them round his studio. When Hartley saw them, they brought back happy memories of his own time at the school.

He was greeted by Jack Lawson, who took him to his office. There hung two identical paintings of a moorland scene and farmstead by Harry Harper.

"Now, Blake," said Jack, pointing to the paintings. "Can you tell me which one of those is the fake? Look carefully."

Hartley looked hard; then shook his head. "No," he replied. "They're identical. Which one is the real thing?"

Jack pointed to one of the paintings. "This one," he said and handed Hartley a magnifying glass. "Look at the right-hand corner of the painting – at those clouds against a blue sky."

Hartley examined the painting closely, then switched his attention to the fake. "The brushwork in those clouds goes the other way in the fake," he said at length.

"Exactly," said Jack. "I suspect the forger is left-handed. Much of his brushwork goes from left to right; whereas Harry Harper was right-handed and his brushwork goes the opposite way. Not always, but in general. There are other differences, too. Notice how the forger has put a small attic window in the farmhouse which isn't there in the original – almost as if he's leaving his personal signature on the painting."

Hartley stood looking at the two paintings a little longer, taking in the details. "Any idea who the forger is?" he asked.

The other shrugged his shoulders. "No, but he has a ready market for his work in America. It was only by chance that I let on them here, when a client brought one in which he'd picked up at a car-boot sale."

"How much is the original worth?" asked Hartley.

"Around twenty thousand pounds," Lawson replied.

The inspector gave a soft laugh. "The Catholics will have done well out of him as one of their priests. As far as I know he'd no relatives." Then he turned back to the painting and said as he left, "Keep your ear to the ground, Jack, and let me know at once if you hear anything about these forgeries. I've a hunch he's someone local."

## CHAPTER THREE

Det. Sgt Ibrahim Khan was paying a visit to the Albert Hotel in Bradford owned by his old school-friend, Feisal Amran, who'd gone into the hotel trade straight from school at fifteen. The bright lad of the class, Ibrahim Khan, had won a place to the local grammar school and then gone up to Oxford, where he'd taken a First in his degree. He'd also won a Blue at golf, much to the chagrin of his new boss, Superintendent Donaldson, a Cambridge graduate.

Yet there was no edge on Khan. He'd retained friendships with old friends from primary schooldays and Feisal Amran was one of them. Khan wasn't to know it was to stand him in good stead as a detective later on in life.

The Pakistani community in Bradford was tightly knit and, like any friendly community, they gossiped among themselves. They knew all about the good and the bad in their midst, and much of the latter revolved round the Quereshi family. The brothers turned to crime at an early age. Over the years, two of them, including Imram the eldest, had been killed in underworld feuds, and Abdul, the next brother in line, was now their leader.

They frequented the Albert Hotel regularly and were there when Ibrahim Khan went in to chat with his friend who served him his coffee at the counter. "I see the Quereshis still come here," he said to Feisal, nodding towards the table where the Quereshis sat.

"They gather here most mornings about now," said Feisal.

"Aren't you worried they might give the place a bad name?" said Khan.

"As long as they don't cause trouble, they can come when they like," replied the other. "I don't really know why they've chosen to come. They know they're not particularly welcome here – or anywhere else."

"It's your coffee," said Khan, smiling and sipping his own drink. "It's the best in Bradford."

"As a matter of fact, Abdul Quereshi was asking after you just before you came. He wants to speak with you urgently," said Feisal, leaning over the counter and lowering his voice.

"He can always contact me at Keighworth police station," said Khan

The other smiled wryly. "A cop-shop is the last place he wants to be seen in," he said. "Anyhow, he's coming over now." And as Quereshi sidled up, Feisal moved to the other end of the bar.

"As-salamu alaykum," he began with the traditional Muslim greeting. Khan returned his greeting and asked him what he wanted. Quereshi looked nervously around and said, "I need your advice."

"As a policeman?" asked Khan. "Or what?"

Quereshi couldn't look Khan in the eye for long and spoke to a point somewhere over Khan's shoulder. "I'm not happy with a certain merchant banker who's employing me," he began.

"Oh? Which shady pie have you got your fingers into this time, Quereshi?" asked Khan.

"There's no need to be sarcastic," said the other, who licked his lips nervously. "The honest truth is I didn't know what I was letting myself in for when I struck a deal with him – international terrorism."

Sgt Khan looked hard at him and realised he was telling the truth. Quereshi was running scared.

"I've been tricked into something I can't get out of, something which isn't my scene at all. You know me well enough to understand I wouldn't be involved with terrorists. I stick to my own patch here in Bradford."

"Where you cause enough trouble. Why come to me?" asked Khan.

"Because I know you. You're the only copper I trust," said Quereshi.

Khan gave a quiet laugh at the irony of the situation, then sipped his coffee before replying. "I don't know about that. What do you want to trust me with?"

Quereshi drew up his stool and looked over his shoulder. "I'm opening a new kebab restaurant in Skipworth, right next to our property agency office. A couple of shops there have been empty for some time and are up for grabs. I thought it ideal to convert them into one restaurant next to our office, but I needed capital so I approached a merchant banker whose name I was given."

"Robin Wilkins?" guessed Khan.

"The same," Quereshi replied, then hesitated before continuing. "He said he'd fund us but there'd be strings attached." And Quereshi looked more worried than ever, explaining how Wilkins had been requested to provide an Urdu-speaking escort for lorries carrying textile equipment to a large weaving complex he was investing in at Jalalabad, near the Afghan border. "I know the area well because some of my family come from there," he continued, "so I agreed to do it and have done one run already." He paused and lit a cigarette. Khan noticed his hand was shaking.

"Go on," encouraged Khan.

"I thought we were taking only equipment, but when the people out there began unloading I realised the lorries had secret compartments – full of arms and ammunition for the Taliban over the border. And Wilkins has been asked by the directors of the complex to take out another load next month."

Ibrahim Khan sensed he was telling the truth for once. Quereshi was running scared and it showed on his face. Khan asked him how Wilkins, a respectable merchant banker, had become involved.

"He's invested heavily in textile engineering in Keighworth, and I was paid well to get together a team of drivers to take loads of textile loom parts by road to Jalalabad on the Afghan border. It's a dangerous run but I've got relatives among the tribes-folk up there and I speak their lingo. So I had a safe passage."

"I see," said Khan thoughtfully. "Have you told anyone else about this?"

Quereshi gave a weak smile. "What's the point? You're the only copper who can help me."

"I don't know about that," said Khan. "But I believe you. Leave it with me, Quereshi."

The other mumbled his thanks then returned to his table. Sgt Khan finished his drink, wished his friend good-bye, then left, nodding at Quereshi on his way out.

When he arrived back in Keighworth, he told Hartley all about his meeting with Quereshi.

"I'll contact Special Branch," said Hartley. "I've one or two contacts there from my time in the army." Blake Hartley had served in the Intelligence Corps during his National Service in the 1950s. Some of those he'd served with had later joined the Foreign Office and gone into Special Branch. Over the years he'd built up a network of useful contacts – unlike his new boss, Superintendent Arthur Donaldson who was still wet behind the ears. He barely knew what routine policing was all about, let alone sophisticated intelligence work.

As it happened, Hartley was due for some leave, and he and his wife Mary decided to go for a short break in London. They stayed in a small bed-and-breakfast in Chelsea and travelled into town each day, sightseeing and going to shows in the evening. They also toured several art galleries and, in one gallery on the King's Road, Hartley saw a painting by his old art master, Harry Harper. It was among a set of provincial artists' works which were for sale.

It was a painting of the old Methodist Chapel on Silegsdene Moor, where Blake's mother's family had worshipped in the past. They'd farmed a nearby smallholding. Hartley examined the painting, knowing what he now knew about the Harper forgeries. Sure enough, when he'd scrutinised it closely it turned out to be a fake.

"How do you know it's not genuine?" asked Mary.

"See the brushwork on the chapel, love?" he said. "It goes from left to right mainly. The same with the sky above the chapel."

Mary looked closer then asked, "So what?"

"It's been painted by a left-handed artist and Harper was right-handed," replied Blake knowledgeably. Mary was impressed. But he came clean. "I learned that from Jack Lawson. He had two identical paintings in his studio, and showed me which one was a fake and how it differed slightly from the other."

"I see," said Mary, looking more closely at the painting again.

The shop assistant saw their interest in the painting and came over. "Can I help you?" she asked.

"No. But you can help yourself," said Blake Hartley straight out.

The assistant looked puzzled so he explained, "You have a fake here.

This painting is a forgery."

The assistant looked even more puzzled and was about to say they didn't display forgeries, when the inspector explained all and showed his ID card. "My wife and I are on holiday in London from Yorkshire. We dropped in here to look over your exhibition and saw this painting alleged to be by Harry Harper who was my old art master. When I looked at it closely I saw it was a fake. There's a forger making copies of Harry Harper's works and raking in a fortune from them. Of course, it's a criminal offence and we're investigating it."

The assistant thanked him and said she'd let the director of the gallery know; meanwhile she called over a porter who took the painting from the display to a store-room. "It's not the first time we've shown a fake here unknowingly. In the art world even experts can be conned. But we always try to exhibit genuine works of art. Thank you so much for your help."

Hartley asked what would happen to the forgery and how they'd come by it.

"It will be returned to the dealer who sent it to us for display and we'll explain why we're sending it back," said the assistant.

"I'd like his name and address," said Hartley.

"Of course," she replied, and led the Hartleys to her office where she gave them the card of the dealer. Hartley glanced at it but didn't recognise the name. The card had a Leeds address on it and he'd check it out when he returned home.

A couple of days later, Blake Hartley and Mary went to Covent Garden Opera House for a performance of 'La Bohème'. They were both keen singers and members of Keighworth Vocal Union so were looking forward to the opera. They thoroughly enjoyed the performance and in the interval went to the bar for a drink.

They were commenting on the opera when a smooth voice behind Hartley said, "It's Inspector Hartley, isn't it?" And turning, the inspector found himself face to face with Robin Wilkins, accompanied by a much younger woman.

He looked relaxed and happy, and the only reference he made to his wife's death was to enquire if there'd been any further developments. He'd heard that her death might not have been suicide.

"I can't envisage it being otherwise," he said, reading Hartley's face. "The case appeared cut and dried when I saw what poor Lucinda had done. She'd been depressed for some time." Then he changed the subject abruptly and introduced the Hartleys to the pretty young blonde accompanying him. "Let me introduce you to my personal assistant, Cheryl. Like me, she's an opera fan so I'm treating her to the performance here tonight. She's earned it because she's a hard worker, eh?" And here he smiled benignly at the girl by his side. They shook hands and Hartley saw that Cheryl fitted into the picture after what the newsagent, Freddy Greenwood, had told him about Wilkins having a dolly bird.

Cheryl flashed a dazzling smile, which she seemed to be able to switch on and off at will. She was attractively dressed in an outfit showing her to her best advantage. Wilkins obviously paid her well and got a good return on his investment.

Meeting Wilkins had cast a bit of a cloud over the Hartleys' night out, and the longer they chatted, the more Hartley took a dislike to him. The banker was patronising. He insisted on paying for their drinks and on their going to his apartment afterwards. His chauffeur would drive them back to their own lodgings later.

Blake Hartley thanked him but said it would be too late, as Wilkins would surely have to face a busy day at work the next day. But the truth was Hartley had had enough of the man and wanted rid. To his consternation, however, Mary said, "Of course we'll come. It'll round the evening off nicely, won't it, Blake?"

Wilkins beamed and Cheryl flashed her alluring smile again. Hartley stood by helpless and had to go along with Mary. But when they returned to their seats, he asked her why she'd agreed to go back to Wilkins' place.

"You're the one who's the sleuth," she said, smiling sweetly. "The more you find out about him, the more you're likely to discover how his wife died. There's a great deal about that man which doesn't ring true. Know thine enemy, Blake!" Her husband pecked her on the cheek and said, "You're quite right, my love – as always." Then they settled down to enjoy the rest of the opera.

When the opera ended, they met Wilkins and his girl in the foyer before driving back to his apartment in Cheapside; and his luxury pad certainly wasn't cheap. It was in the top bracket of London property.

It occupied the entire ground floor of a luxury block and had a large courtyard and garage attached. There, Wilkins kept his silver Rolls Royce and two expensive sports cars. And the whole place was tightly ringed with security precautions, so tight it felt oppressive.

An electric fence ran round the courtyard, where guards patrolled 24/7. They were supervised by the chauffeur, who, despite his tailored uniform and smart hat, still looked like a bouncer. His nose was at odds with the rest of his face and he had cabbage ears pinned either side of a coarse face.

Inside the apartment Blake and his wife couldn't help but be impressed by the expensive antiques and costly paintings hanging on the walls. Among them was a Harper water-colour of a moorland scene above Keighworth. It complemented a Constable of the Essex countryside which hung next to it. Hartley was drawn to it at once. It was genuine, like the adjacent Constable.

"Rather a contrast, don't you think – Constable and Harper?"

commented Wilkins who'd strolled over, leaving Cheryl to pour the drinks. "Two very different men coming from very different backgrounds, yet both of them great artists."

"Indeed," replied Hartley, as they re-joined the ladies to be served their drinks and make small talk.

"So," began Wilkins, "how's your London holiday going?"

"Excellently," Mary answered. "There's always so much to do and see. But you'll know all about that working down here as a banker. Tell me Mr Wilkins..."

"Do call me Robin," interrupted Wilkins.

"Tell me, Robin," she continued, smiling sweetly back at him, "what exactly does a merchant banker do?" And all the while Blake stood by listening and enjoying his whisky with the quiet interrogation his wife was carrying out on her host.

"First and foremost he's a gambler," began the banker heartily, then more seriously, "He's a man – or woman – who's accumulated capital then invests it in a variety of enterprises. In other words he makes a calculated gamble investing in new companies he thinks will prosper. Those companies can be here or overseas. And when the right time comes, he sells his share in the companies; hopefully at a good profit."

"But how is that different from high-street banking?" asked Mary.

"The risks are greater, especially when you help exporters hedge against fluctuating markets overseas. The biggest problem is getting enough capital together to get started," he replied.

"And how does a potential merchant banker find the capital to kick-start his bank?" continued Mary, leading him on.

Wilkins swirled the brandy round his glass and looked into it before meeting Mary's eye. "Oh," he said thoughtfully, "by various means. He can pool his capital with colleagues who chip in their share then take their share of profits; or he may inherit his starting capital from various sources."

"And you?" persisted Mary. "How did you accrue your capital, if I may ask?"

Wilkins took another swig of his brandy before answering. "My first wife, Sandra, was left quite a bit of money by her father. She helped me get started. I owe a lot to poor Sandra," he said, then added quietly, "She was a wonderful wife – so was Lucinda till this tragedy happened."

He seemed upset so Mary quickly changed the subject. More about his banking practices would come out later. But Mary's questions confirmed what Blake Hartley had suspected. Wilkins had amassed his wealth by marrying two rich heiresses. Both marriages had ended tragically and mysteriously.

The banker's final comment was, "All life's a gamble, y'know. You win some and you lose some." Then he finished off his brandy and asked Cheryl to re-fill his glass and those of his guests.

They didn't stay long after that; just long enough for Robin Wilkins to show off his expensive furniture and paintings, the fruits of merchant banking he said smiling broadly. His chauffeur drove the Hartleys to their lodgings, leaving him to enjoy the company and delights of Cheryl for the rest of the night – another of his banking perks.

## CHAPTER FOUR

A few days after his London jaunt, Inspector Hartley paid a visit to the drop-in centre near Keighworth parish church. It was run by volunteers for the homeless and poor, and was housed in an old school-room where the volunteers served hot drinks and food throughout the day. It closed only when the night-shelter opened. Also manned by volunteers, the night-shelter was funded by the church in the town and provided accommodation for the homeless who wanted a bed for the night. Many, however, preferred to sleep rough in derelict houses or under the table-tombs in the church graveyard, weather permitting.

A regular client at the drop-in centre was 'Smarmy' Williams, who got his name from the shady dealings he dabbled in. An earlier generation would have called him a 'spiv'; such men ran the black market in wartime austerity, but now in the post-war world dabbled in drug-dealing and fencing stolen goods.

Once inside the drop-in centre, Hartley picked up his cup of tea then joined a group at their table. He noticed Smarmy chatting *sotto voce* to a group the other side of the room. When Hartley entered, Smarmy was about to show the group something he'd taken from his large overcoat; but when he saw the inspector, he hurriedly put it back. However, it didn't escape Hartley's eagle eye and he asked the man sitting next to him what Smarmy was up to.

"He's into everything is Smarmy, boss," the other said. "I hear he's flogging paintings now."

Hartley was all ears at once. "What sort of paintings?" he asked.

"Local. Some guy who was a teacher in town I heard."

"Harry Harper?" asked Hartley.

"Aye. That's the one, boss," the other replied. "Why? D'you know him?"

"He was my art master at school," said Hartley. "His paintings go for thousands now. I saw one for sale in London last week, but it was a fake. "Hartley sipped his tea then said thoughtfully more to himself than the other, "So Smarmy is selling Harper paintings now."

When he'd finished his tea, he strolled over to Smarmy Williams' table. Smarmy saw him coming and got up to leave, but the inspector blocked his way and said, "I'd like a word with you, Smarmy, before you go. Let's talk where it's less crowded." And putting his hand on the other's shoulder he steered him to an empty table and told him to sit down.

"What's up, boss?" pleaded Smarmy, coming the innocent. "What d'you want to talk to me about? I've done nowt wrong."

Hartley smiled. "I'm sure you haven't, Smarmy. I simply want to ask you about the paintings you're selling."

"Harry Harper's?" said Smarmy. "What about them? I haven't nicked 'em. All I do is act as go-between for the bloke what's selling 'em an' earn commission on the ones I sell. It's all above board, boss."

"And where do you sell them?" asked Hartley.

"Whoever'll have 'em – art galleries, collectors. If somebody wants one, I'll sell it. There's good money in paintings by Harry Harper. Folks'll pay a fortune for one these days," said Smarmy, relieved that Hartley hadn't touched on any of his other shady deals.

Hartley knew this and kept up his line of enquiry. "Who supplies you with the paintings, Smarmy?" he asked.

Smarmy lit a cigarette and drew heavily on it as he weighed his reply. "If I tell you, you won't say I did, boss?" he said finally, blowing a cloud of smoke into the air.

"I never disclose names given in confidence – even by crooks," said Hartley firmly.

Smarmy drew his chair closer and lowered his voice. "The guy I get them from is called Raymond Lester. I sell Harper paintings from my shop in the market. He brings them to me there, but I don't know where he gets them from. Honest, boss."

Hartley looked hard at him. He was telling the truth. The shop was where Smarmy ran his house-clearance business – and other more dubious dealings. He fenced stolen goods there but always had an alibi when questioned by the police. He was small-time, but a useful copper's nark, helping the police when they were after bigger fish.

After more questioning, they walked round the corner to Smarmy's shop. He said he was expecting Raymond Lester to bring another painting that day. Smarmy's place was in a row of grubby single-storey shops thrown up years before and now very dilapidated. It was wedged between a cycle shop and a second-hand clothes shop.

Its frontage boasted a large notice-board announcing house-clearance as the shop's speciality; nothing too large or too small; everything cleared. A display of furniture filled the window. Behind was ranged a variety of items: crockery, pots and pans, rugs, carpets and other household goods. Outside, more durable bits and pieces were on display including a couple of wash-stands and some enamel tubs. They joined the furniture inside each night when the shop closed.

Inside was Smarmy's assistant, a shifty-eyed, young man very like Smarmy himself. He was flashily dressed in a natty, double-breasted suit with a loud tie. His shoes were highly polished, patterned and pointed. He'd a pimply face but his speech was as smooth as butter.

He greeted his boss with a smile which faded when he recognised Inspector Hartley. Panic flitted across his face momentarily, but he soon recovered and wished his boss and Hartley good-day.

"Inspector Hartley's come to check out the paintings on display," explained Smarmy, giving the assistant a meaningful look.

"Come this way, sir," said the assistant, standing back to let Hartley pass into a grubby back-room, where more furniture and paintings were stored. Among the latter were a couple of Harry Harper water colours, well priced as were some prints of them.

"You do a good trade in Harper paintings, I see," observed the inspector, going to the paintings.

"He's become very popular," said the assistant, "especially with the Americans."

"I've managed to get them hung in a London gallery, where I sell most of the originals, but the prints go well here. We act as agents for the London gallery," added Williams.

Hartley asked how he'd become the agent for Harper's works.

"An art-collector bought some furniture from us and noticed we sold paintings. He mentioned he'd a set of Harper paintings he wanted to sell and was looking for an agency to take them on. He'd bought them cheaply while Harry Harper was still alive before he became famous. Of course, I jumped at the opportunity and became the agent.

As a matter of fact, Mr Lester phoned me only this morning to say he'd another Harper for sale. He'll be bringing it here any time now," said Smarmy, looking at his watch.

"I'll wait for him," said Hartley, and browsed round the shop till Lester appeared.

Raymond Lester was about the same age as Hartley, in his late fifties and going grey. He had a bushy moustache, a left-over from his time in the army, where he'd been a sergeant-major. He was accompanied by his wife, Edith, a quiet little woman who let her husband do all the talking as he unwrapped the painting he'd brought. It was a painting of the parish church in the village where Harper had lived.

Lester held it up on the counter for Hartley and Williams to look at. They both stood silent a moment, Hartley rubbing his chin before stepping forward to have a closer view. He studied it a while, then asked Lester where he'd got the painting from.

He gave Hartley a keen look before replying cautiously, "I have a collection of them. I knew him when he was alive. I live in Silegsdene and used to see him often sketching in the village and the countryside around."

Leaving Hartley and Lester talking about Harper, Smarmy sidled out of the room to join his assistant. He suspected what was coming and didn't want to be involved.

Once they were alone, Inspector Hartley showed Lester his ID and said who he was. "I'd like to know where you're getting these forgeries from," he said quietly.

"Forgeries!" exclaimed Lester, but before he could say more, his wife intervened. She'd looked more and more agitated all the while she'd been there.

"Tell him the truth, Raymond. We were bound to be found out sooner or later. Tell him about our Michael."

Lester looked across at her angrily a moment then calmed down and said, "You're right, love. Better now than later when things may be worse. Come to our place, inspector, and I'll explain everything."

On his way out, Hartley thanked Smarmy Williams for showing him round; then added casually at the door, "Oh, will you put those Harper paintings to one side, please? I'll want them as evidence before long."

"Evidence!" exclaimed the other. "Why?"

"That'll be apparent in time. Meanwhile, take good care of them."

"If you say so, boss," said Smarmy looking crestfallen. He was doing very well out of Harry Harper, thank you.

Hartley and the Lesters left with the painting they'd brought with them. They lived in a bungalow in Ruddledene, a suburb built in the 1930s. The houses were more up-market than the terraced houses in town, but not quite as exclusive as the mini-mansions at Utworth. You were on your way up when you lived in Ruddledene. You'd arrived when you bought a house in Utworth.

The bungalow was well maintained and had a large garden with a shed where the Lesters' son, Michael, lived and had his studio. He was no mean artist as Hartley was soon to discover.

Sadly, he was very autistic and entirely dependent on his parents, his only contact with the outside world. He was nearly forty and unmarried and lived all day in the shed with his paints and easels; leaving his studio only to eat or gossip with his mother and father.

He was a big young man, a shade over six feet tall and well built. He was good-looking, too, and in the normal way of things would have had a girl-friend or been married. But he was inordinately shy and withdrawn, leaving all the talking in company to his parents. Usually, when visitors came he retired to his shed.

When they were in the shed, his father explained all. "It's like this, inspector. Michael had no job. He can't work with others. But he's a genius working by himself, painting and drawing. You see, he's autistic and his only income was from benefits till I began selling his paintings."

The father did all the talking while his wife, Edith, and their son remained silent. It was Raymond Lester who was his son's agent and the go-between with Smarmy Williams. "When I realised what talent he had and that we had a ready market for his work at Mr Williams' place, the temptation was too great. We needed the cash badly so I set him on copying Harry Harper's work," he continued.

"Does he paint originals?" asked Hartley, glancing round the shed.

"Yes, but they make nothing like the amount we get for his forgeries," said Lester, looking more and more ill at ease. "You see how it is. If there's any blame in all this, it's mine. Michael has no idea what's going on."

Inspector Hartley turned to the son and asked him if he'd anything to say. He shook his head and Hartley didn't pursue the conversation with him. But he did request Michael's signature on the notes he'd made and Hartley noticed he used his left hand – as in the forged paintings.

That done, he turned back to the father and said, "I'm glad you came clean, Mr Lester. It'll save a great deal of trouble all round, but I shall have to charge your son with forgery and you with aiding and abetting. You'll both have to appear in court."

"Will they go to prison?" asked Edith, fearfully.

"I don't know," Hartley answered, "but as a full admission of guilt has been made the sentence should be more lenient than if you'd tried to cover up." Hartley looked round the displayed paintings and said, "It's a great pity you did this, Mr Lester. Your son has talent. He's a great artist in his own right."

Michael Lester listened in silence and said nothing when Hartley cautioned him. It was one of the occasions when he felt deeply for the man he was arresting.

Yet it all worked out much as Hartley had surmised when the case went to court. The judge took into account Michael Lester's condition and told him gently but firmly he must not fake any more Harper paintings. He imposed a fine and gave a suspended sentence on both father and son. Raymond Lester was told he would go straight to prison if he sold any more fake paintings and Smarmy Williams was ordered to hand over all the forgeries he held for burning.

Hartley was relieved by the judgement. His role as priest sometimes was at odds with his role as policeman. However, there was a happy outcome to the Lester case. Some months later, Raymond Lester phoned to ask if Hartley would arrange to meet him privately and Hartley arranged to see him at the café where he had his morning coffee. When they met, Lester presented Hartley with a painting done specially by his son for the inspector, a painting of Ingerworth parish church, where Hartley was a non-stipendiary minister.

It was a superb piece of work and Hartley said he'd hang it in the church. He asked how Michael Lester was faring. "He's making a name for himself in the world of art under his own name," said the father proudly. "He's had a recent break-through onto the London art scene. He's being exhibited at a gallery in Kings Road, Chelsea. Smarmy Williams recommended his work there. It's selling like hot cakes; and the gallery has signed up for more."

## CHAPTER FIVE

In the latter half of the twentieth century Keighworth shed some of its Victorian buildings and gave itself a facelift with a new glass-covered market place and town centre. Sadly, its splendid Edwardian theatre was sacrificed to modernity, but thankfully the Victorian main streets remained intact, unlike those in numerous nearby towns, such as Bradford. The fine Carnegie Library and the renowned Cycling Club block were left untouched for future generations to enjoy.

Blake Hartley sometimes took his morning coffee break outside under the new glass canopy over the market. He was there one morning with Ibrahim Khan when Robin Wilkins strolled by, accompanied by Abdul Quereshi! It was hard to say who was the more surprised when they met, but Khan and Quereshi kept quiet about knowing each other when Wilkins introduced Quereshi.

"Well, well, well, this is a surprise, inspector. Let me introduce you to one of my business colleagues, Mr Quereshi," he began, then after the handshakes he continued. "Inspector Hartley and Sgt Khan investigated the sad death of my wife."

They shook hands and Hartley invited them to join him and his sergeant. He was curious why Quereshi and Wilkins were so closely connected, knowing as he did Quereshi's past. There was more to this man than mere banking. A dark side to his past was beginning to emerge: the death of two wealthy wives, and now this association with a known criminal.

Wilkins explained at some length his business connection with Quereshi, who maintained his pose with Khan; but the longer they chatted – or rather the longer Wilkins chatted, for he was a great talker – the more ill at ease Quereshi looked. It didn't escape either of the detectives' notice. He was hardly the willing associate Wilkins made him out to be.

"You see," explained Wilkins, "I've invested heavily in a new textile complex in Pakistan, on the Afghan border not far from the Khyber pass. An ideal location in many ways and it will employ several hundred workers, where work is badly needed. In fact, it will create a new community there. Do you know that part of the world, sergeant?"

"Tribal territory," said Khan. "A bit out of my way. My family comes from Karachi."

"How interesting," said Wilkins. "That's where I have my base. Mr Quereshi arranges transport of equipment manufactured here in Keighworth then exported to Pakistan. It's stored at my base in Karachi before going up to Jalalabad on the border. It's all financed by my bank. A bit of a gamble but I know it'll pay off in time."

Sgt Khan glanced across at Quereshi, but he wouldn't meet his eye. He looked nervous. He was into something he couldn't handle and he contacted Khan later to tell him he'd been tricked into something far worse than he imagined. He was unwittingly gun-running for Wilkins under the pretence of driving out lorry-loads of textile equipment for the new plant. In reality, Wilkins was in cahoots with the Taliban and tribesmen who controlled the borderlands between Afghanistan and Pakistan and selling them arms.

Meanwhile, Wilkins chatted on about his banking affairs. His life was totally wrapped up in making money. As Hartley found out the longer he knew him, he'd stoop to anything to gain more wealth and was completely amoral. "Beyond redemption", he told his wife Mary when they were discussing the case later.

Before they left, Khan was able to take Quereshi to one side and speak with him alone. He clearly wanted a word in private and told the sergeant that Wilkins had asked him to take another load of machinery to Jalalabad, which meant another long, hazardous journey from Karachi through the Afghan border country. The journey by road was bad enough, but made much worse by the tribesmen and others they encountered en route.

On their way back to the police station, Sgt Khan told Hartley what Quereshi had said. They decided to tell their new boss, Superintendent Arthur Donaldson, who was taken completely by surprise. He'd never expected anything like this, for he'd little experience of routine police work, never mind being involved with something which might involve the Foreign Office or MI5. It threw him into a complete panic.

After they'd told him, he stood up, biting his lip and jingling the loose change in his trouser pocket. Then he looked out of the window as if seeking inspiration from the pigeons in Town Hall Square. After a few moments he turned back to the inspector and sergeant and said in a small voice, "What do you suggest we do?"

Blake Hartley, who'd been in the Intelligence Corps during his National Service, said, "I suggest you contact Special Branch, sir. They'll put you in touch with the Foreign Office and MI5."

Donaldson blenched. It was all becoming too much for him. "And then?" he almost whispered.

"I expect they'll brief Sgt Khan what to do if they're going to involve him, and I've no doubt they will. It's a golden opportunity to get an undercover agent in on the scene and find out more about the deals Wilkins is doing with the Taliban. Once they've enough evidence to nail him, they'll pounce," said Hartley smiling quietly before continuing, "A good beginning to your time here, sir."

Donaldson perked up. He already had his eye on his next promotion. Keighworth was but a stepping-stone in his career, preferably back down south in the Home Counties where he'd been born and raised.

"You're quite right, Hartley," he said, looking more confident. "It is a challenge - a challenge we must all rise to." The prospect of a successful counter-terrorist operation on his patch cheered him immensely.

And so Det. Sgt Ibrahim Khan, travelling under an assumed name, was given the go-ahead to work undercover for Special Branch as escort to Quereshi. They were ostensibly transporting textile machinery from Karachi to Jalalabad on the Afghan frontier, a wild region controlled by the Taliban and native tribesmen.

They stayed overnight in Karachi at Wilkins' apartment near one of the city beaches at Hawke's Bay. Wilkins also had an office in the financial sector of the city, where he carried out his business transactions and met clients – a very shady lot, indeed.

They left Karachi at daybreak one morning, but already the roads were jammed with traffic: cars, lorries, bicycles and hundreds of motor bikes laden with passengers and luggage. Though it was scarcely light the city buzzed with life and noise. Khan and Quereshi spoke little. When they did it was to comment on some passing activity and the congestion, which made Bradford look like a quiet country village.

The lorry had been loaded by Wilkins' men before they arrived at the warehouse where the banker stored the parts for the textile complex he was financing. And much more as Khan was to discover.

Thrust as he was so suddenly into the situation he now was in, Khan felt he was living out a dream, an unreal situation; acting under cover abroad with an assumed name as co-driver to a criminal he'd known from boyhood. Since his return to Yorkshire, their paths had crossed several times. Abdul Quereshi was the eldest son of a large family, all of whom had turned to crime. Several had gone to prison, but Abdul had never been caught. He was a wily bird and cloaked his crime with apparent model citizenship. His brothers and others had always taken the rap, while he built up thriving businesses in the restaurant trade and land agency to front his crimes.

By contrast, though brought up in the same area, Ibrahim Khan had come from a hard-working family. His parents had given him every opportunity to make good in life. He'd won a place at a local grammar school, where he'd done well before being awarded a bursary to Oxford University. There he'd taken a First in Greats and gone to police college after graduation. He'd also won a Blue for golf at Oxford, much to the envy of Superintendent Donaldson, a keen golfer and Cambridge graduate.

So here he was now with a scared crook he'd known all his life, driving into the wild badlands of northern Pakistan, transporting goodness knew what up-country to Jalalabad.

Khan learned much about Wilkins as they drove through the most rugged and hostile frontier territory. Although he and Quereshi were both of Pakistani stock, they felt like foreigners in their forebears' country. They were stopped frequently as they passed tribal frontiers, or when the Taliban checked them out. Wilkins had given them the password "tiger" to get through. It acted like magic and they were allowed to continue their slow journey to Jalalabad.

Their journey took them through some of the wildest and toughest territory in the whole country. The roads were badly maintained and rutted, so they couldn't go at any speed but crawled along. Near Quetta they were stopped by an army patrol, itself venturing into alien territory, risking an attack any time by hostile tribesmen. There was an unwritten pact between them and the military. If either of them broke it they were attacked by the other.

The officer asked to see their identity cards and then searched their cargo. The arms and ammunition they carried were well hidden behind a sealed compartment. However, he asked for money claiming it was a levy on all goods vehicles travelling along that route. It was a bribe, but Quereshi paid up. He knew the routine.

They didn't have to pay out again, for the Taliban and the tribesmen knew what was in the lorry. On the odd occasion when they were stopped, the password 'tiger' magicked them through at once. Wilkins had set up a system which ran like clockwork. He supplied textile machinery to the directors of the plant he was investing in, and the Taliban and tribesmen received arms and ammunition. In return they supplied him with heroin from the poppy fields which he distributed in Europe through his contacts there.

However, there was a scary incident when Khan and Quereshi finally arrived at the mills. Following instructions, they remained in the cab while equipment was unloaded by men from the mill. That done, the lorry was left in the car-park to await the arrival of the Taliban, who knew where their arms were hidden. But before they came, some Pashtun tribesmen turned up demanding their share of the weaponry they knew was in the lorry.

They were a wild-looking bunch, who ordered Khan and Quereshi out of their cab, threatening to kill them if they didn't say where the weapons were hidden. They said they didn't know and the Pashtuns were just about to start taking the lorry apart to find the weapons when the Taliban appeared. The tribesmen fled.

The Taliban knew exactly how to dismantle the lorry and recover the weapons. Within minutes they'd emptied the secret compartment of its weaponry, replacing it with plastic bags full of heroin. Then they sealed up the compartment once more and went as quickly as they'd come, back into the hills, leaving Quereshi with a large canvas bag stashed with money.

Khan and Quereshi were left wondering what was going to happen next. They went to the manager's office and left the cash-bag with him. He'd pay the money to Wilkins as it was too risky taking it back to Karachi in the lorry. How glad they were to be on the road again heading back to the city and civilisation!

## CHAPTER SIX

While his sergeant was working undercover in Pakistan, Inspector Hartley held the fort at Keighworth. He was very much in charge because the new superintendent was at a loss. What made matters worse was that Donaldson was unaware of his failings and very full of himself. He irritated his inspector more and more. Mary, his wife, sensed this and brought up the subject one evening at dinner.

"How have you gone on today, Blake, with your new boss?" she asked. Her husband was unusually quiet.

"So, so," he replied casually, sipping his tea.

"What do you mean 'so, so'?" she went on, realising all was not right.

"Well, to tell you the truth, love, he's a bit full of himself. Always name-dropping and going on about just being elected a member of the Royal Ridings Golf Club over in Leeds."

Mary smiled. She knew what her husband thought about golf clubs and the pecking orders they had. But Blake tended to keep his feelings to himself. His sergeant was a first-class golfer, and this came in useful at times, as he managed to pick up bits of information relevant to the cases in hand while playing a round of golf.

"Donaldson's got a lot to learn, but I hope he'll settle in as time goes by," continued Hartley.

"Yet as a superintendent you'd have thought he'd have had some experience," said Mary.

Hartley pursed his lips. "Traffic-control in London and office-management. That seems to be about the limit of his experience. I've a feeling he's got to where he is by who he knows – and he knows plenty of people in the right quarters. His sort always do."

"His sort?" echoed Mary.

"The old-school-tie sort. From what he's already told us, he has the right contacts and went to the right school. His dad's a bishop and his wife's dad's a general in the army as he keeps reminding us," said Hartley re-filling his tea-cup.

"Oh, come on, Blake. You've a bit of a chip on your shoulder about public schools and pecking orders. People can't help which class they were born into," said Mary.

"But they've no need to keep letting you know; especially when they've discovered where you started life and what your background was," grumbled her husband.

Mary responded that she hoped her husband was man enough to take all that and his new boss in his stride, and be proud of his own achievements in life. And if all fails, be devious. "Wives have to be devious all the time with blinkered husbands," she added, laughing.

Blake smiled and reached across the table to squeeze her hand. Their marriage was a very happy one despite the odd bit of deviousness to cement it. He took her point and from then on became reconciled to Superintendent Donaldson's self-trumpetings and snobbery.

He met the superintendent the same evening at a Masonic lodge guest night. Hartley went as the guest of an old friend, the forensic pathologist, Dr Gus Dunwell. They sang in the same town choir and acted at times in the local theatre group. Also at the guest night was Robin Wilkins, a fellow mason of the superintendant's.

Just to make the point that he was on close terms with Wilkins, Donaldson invited Hartley to join them at their table for a drink. "Good to see you here, Hartley," he said patronisingly. "I gather you already know Mr Wilkins. He asked me to bring you over for a drink. What will you have?"

Hartley thanked him but declined the offer. He was driving and said he didn't want to lose his licence. This amused Wilkins who laughed heartily.

"Good to know there's a man with a ready wit working on my late wife's case," said Wilkins. "How's it going?" He spoke with no sense of loss; more with concern how Hartley was proceeding with his investigation.

"It's going to take longer than I thought at first," said Hartley.

"How d'you mean?" said Wilkins, looking more apprehensive.

"I can't go into details, sir, but there are several loose ends which need tying up," replied Hartley non-committally; and that left Wilkins looking more worried than ever.

"Such as?" he couldn't help asking.

"I can't say, sir, till our investigations are complete," said Hartley firmly.

"Quite so; quite so," said the other hurriedly, but the worried look on his face wasn't lost on Hartley. Wilkins changed the subject and asked how Hartley found the Monet exhibition in London.

By now, Donaldson felt very much left out of the conversation and the reference to Monet pushed him further to the margin. He was not an art connoisseur – nor was he well read, so he had to stand silent till the conversation gave him an opening; and then he almost blew Sgt Khan's cover.

Wilkins asked how Khan was faring, for he'd met him in Keighworth when Khan was involved in investigating Mrs Wilkins' death.

"He's away from the station at present," began Donaldson, taking his cue.

He would have gone on chattering but Hartley quickly silenced him with, "He's on a course at police college; brushing up for his promotion exams." Then Hartley glared across at his boss, who realised he'd made a gaffe and shut up.

His inspector quickly steered the subject away from Khan and asked how Wilkins' bank was faring. He said it was thriving and he was embarking on a new venture locally, investing in a luxury-car garage just opened in Keighworth.

"Keighworth is having to diversify now that the textile trade is in recession," he said. "Yet people are growing wealthy with the new money floating about. That's why I'm investing in Clymo's Garage, just opened in the Worth Valley Industrial Centre."

"A very astute move, I'd say, Robin," offered Donaldson who was a great car man and knew more about the motor trade than he did about policing.

Inspector Hartley shot him a disdainful glance which didn't escape Wilkins' notice. For all his bluff, businessman-of-the-world act, Wilkins was a shrewd observer of people. He realised quickly that Hartley needed watching. He certainly wasn't the droll plodder his boss made him out to be.

"A very enterprising garage director and that's why I'm investing in it," continued Wilkins.

"Aye," agreed Hartley. "The Clymo brothers are well known in the area. Jack Clymo was a first-class racing driver before he retired. He went all over the world competing."

"And that's exactly why I'm investing in his new garage complex," said Wilkins.

Quick off the mark as ever, Donaldson chipped in with, "Best get him into the Lodge then, Robin. People of his standing are always welcome."

"Good idea, Arthur. I'll invite him and his brother to the next guest night," said Wilkins. "They're just the sort we want in the lodge."

After more chit-chat Hartley re-joined Dr Dunwell and the churchwarden at Ingerworth church, Jack Clapham, who was also a mason. It turned out that Jack was the lawyer involved in the property and land transfer with the new garage complex. In the past, he'd also done business with Robin Wilkins and knew the family background of both his wives.

"That's where he obtained the capital to launch his merchant bank," explained the lawyer confidentially to his friends. And when Hartley asked what Wilkins did prior to merchant banking, Jack Clapham filled him in. "He went into high-street banking straight from school as his dad was manager of the Ridings County Bank in Keighworth. Robin Wilkins did well and in time worked his way up to branch manager. In his thirties he married his first wife, Sandra Butterworth. She was a lot older than him and the widow of a mill magnate, a millionaire several times over whose fortune she inherited. It all passed to Wilkins when she died and it was the capital with which he launched his merchant bank and started investing abroad."

Inspector Hartley listened intently. Jack Clapham certainly gave him something to think about, and he made more discreet enquiries about the deaths of Wilkins' wives. The longer he pursued his investigations, the less the two deaths looked like suicide.

## CHAPTER SEVEN

Sgt Khan, working under the pseudonym of Jangeer Ali as co-driver to Quereshi, was stopped several times by tribesmen on the way back to Karachi; yet each time when they had given the magical password 'tiger' they were allowed to proceed. There was clearly a well-established line of communication between Wilkins' mercenaries and the tribesmen. Only once had they been forced to pay a levy – and that to an army patrol again. Fortunately, the military were absent in the remoter regions. Over the years, they'd been seen off by local tribesmen, who were paid protection money by the poppy-growing local farmers, who were part of a lucrative heroin market.

But when they arrived back in the city things were very different. It was mayhem. Karachi had become home to several million Pashtun refugees, fleeing from Afghanistan about the time the city began to run down. Once it had been the most flourishing port in the region; but that all changed when rival ethnic groups settled in the city and feuds broke out between rival gangs who controlled their own areas.

After their trip, Quereshi was driving his lorry back to Wilkins' warehouse when it was stopped by four gunmen on motorbikes. Two of them opened the door of the cab and pointed their weapons at Quereshi and Khan. They were ordered to leave the cab, then frisked. That done, they were bound and led to a waiting car, which took them to the gang's hideout in another part of the city. There, a ransom was demanded for their release.

Quereshi tried explaining to their captors that he was merely a temporary driver for Wilkins like his co-driver. He said they were working on contract as they knew the border route well.

"Then if you're worth it, your boss will pay up," said the gang leader.

"And if he doesn't?" asked Khan.

The other grinned and said maliciously, "You're expendable." Then he spat on the ground.

Khan asked him who he was. The gang-leader wouldn't give a name but did say he was a Pashtun, like the rest of the gang. They made their living by crime.

He stood near the broken window of the derelict shed they'd taken their prisoners to, and kept looking out constantly into the yard outside. Inside were rusting metal stanchions holding the place up and it was against one of these that Khan and Quereshi were propped with their hands tightly bound behind them.

When the guard went to the other end of the long building to relieve himself, Khan rubbed the rope round his wrists against the rough edge of the stanchion he was tied to. Before the guard came back, he'd severed it and then freed Quereshi.

The guard never knew what hit him when he returned. They bound him with their own bonds and gagged him, leaving him trussed on the floor as they fled back to their truck. There was no sign of the other Pashtuns and they sped off double-quick to Wilkins' warehouse across the city.

They remained there, guarded by Wilkins' heavies till they made their next trip to Jalalabad. This time they went with an escort of armed men. They were taking no chances with the Pashtuns or any other immigrant groups in the city. And after they'd done a couple of more runs and he was afraid his cover might be blown, Sgt Khan returned to Keighworth and resumed his routine work there with Hartley, who in due course heard all about Khan's undercover adventure.

Abdul Quereshi wasn't long following him. It was easier - and safer - being a criminal in Bradford than gun-running in Pakistan. There was law in Bradford, even if he was often on the wrong side of it. Both he and Sgt Khan said nothing about their Karachi adventure till much later.

Meanwhile, Wilkins invested quite a bit in Clymo's Garage, newly opened in the Worth Valley Industrial Centre. He also bought more property in the centre of town, including an up-market restaurant and hair-salon. When Abdul Quereshi returned, Wilkins loaned him money to open a land agency and letting office in Skipworth which Wilkins then used as a cover for some dubious property deals. He kept his tabs on Quereshi right to the end.

The garage he financed in Keighworth was a splendid affair. On the ground floor, it had a large display room, all chromium and glass, which overlooked a courtyard where a large steel model of the Jaguar logo greeted potential buyers as they entered. Gleaming bright on display inside were the most up-to-date models of expensive cars like Jaguars, Rolls Royce and Mercedes. Behind them were the offices where slick salesmen sat picking their teeth and gossiping while they awaited clients.

The more he met him and the more he heard about him, the more Inspector Hartley began to suspect Wilkins was up to no good. When they met, Wilkins was too bland, too smooth, yet patronising; and being patronised irked Hartley more than anything else. He decided one day to pay a visit to Clymo's garage to find out more about Keighworth's banker.

It was unusually fine for Keighworth when he set out. The town spent most of the year under Pennine cloud; if it wasn't actually raining, it was about to. It was some distance to the garage and he had to pass through the industrial heartland of Keighworth, its large engineering works, its woollen mills and railway sidings, till he came to where the old nineteenth century stone buildings were being demolished and replaced with the slick glass and concrete of the twentieth century.

Where some of the older buildings remained the contrast was stark. They were now converted into warehouses and the offices of haulage companies whose lorries were parked outside. The ancient hamlet in the Worth Valley had disappeared and was now given over to garages and haulage.

Hartley strolled past the dazzling display of Jaguars and BMWs and entered the office where a beaming salesman scurried over to him. "Can I help you, sir?" he asked smiling, but the smile evaporated when Hartley showed his ID.

"I'm making some enquiries about the late Mrs Wilkins," he began. "I wondered if anyone here had contact with her around the time she died."

The other thought for a moment then said, "As a matter of fact I called at Mr Wilkins' home that morning with a spare engine part the chauffeur had requested. As I left, I noticed a new Renault with a French number plate parked in the drive outside the house."

"Anyone in it?" asked Hartley.

"No, but at the time I guessed that whoever was driving it had gone into the house," said the other.

"You're quite sure of the date," said Hartley.

"Positive. I've logged my visit in my office diary," said the salesman pointing to a diary on his desk.

They chatted some more and before he left Hartley said how impressed he was with the new garage. It must have involved considerable outlay.

"Mr Clymo has spared no expense," said the salesman. "Only the best will do for him. In our line of business you can't afford to cut corners."

"And he pays you well also?" offered Hartley smiling.

Encouraged, the smile slid back onto the salesman's face. "He's a caring employer," he offered, but didn't comment further; nor did he offer to show the inspector round the place after he knew he was from the police.

When Hartley left, he walked back into the centre of town, where he dropped in at the Lotus restaurant for coffee. Its owner was one of his parishioners, whose name was Harry Hung Wo, an immigrant from Hong Kong years before.

He was a very sociable Chinese national who'd settled well in Keighworth; so well, he knew all that was going on in town, all the gossip and scandal. He was a regular worshipper at Ingerworth church and Hartley often called at the restaurant for coffee when he was passing. He said Harry made the best coffee in town, and the detective sometimes picked up scraps of useful information. He learned much that day about Robin Wilkins and the recent properties he'd bought in Keighworth, the Mayfair restaurant and Pauli's hair salon, said to be the best in Keighworth – and the most expensive.

"I've heard along the grapevine that there's more than food being served at the Mayfair restaurant, and more than hair being styled at Pauli's hair salon," said Harry when they settled down to their drink.

"Oh?" said Hartley putting down his cup. "What else is going on?"

"It's only hearsay, mind you, from one of my kitchen staff," continued Harry. "But he's heard that clients at both places are heroin addicts supplied by Wilkins' pushers."

"A dash of smack with your coffee or perm, eh?" said Hartley whimsically as he finished his drink. "And I suspect I know where it's coming from. There's much more to Mr Wilkins than meets the eye. He stores all sorts of dubious goods under his bank counter and has some very dodgy clients."

## CHAPTER EIGHT

"Concrete data and pre-operational research method," began Superintendent Arthur Donaldson, glancing down at the notes before him. He was holding a regular staff-training session which he'd instituted since his appointment. Bored to tears along with the rest of the staff forced to attend were Inspector Hartley and Sgt Khan.

Only Detective Constable Kempton, who'd arrived about the same time as Donaldson, listened attentively to what the boss was saying and took notes. Like the boss he was ambitious and wanted promotion. Consequently he became the superintendent's blue-eyed boy, whereas Hartley and the rest were regarded as stick-in-the-muds who needed up-dating. Donaldson saw that as the very first priority in his new post.

He went on at some length, expanding "concrete data" and "pre-operational research method", well laced with more jargon of similar ilk. When he'd ended his talk his yawning audience knew exactly where they stood with him and what sort of person their new boss was.

"Know what I think?" said Hartley to Khan when they'd returned to the office they shared.

"I can guess, sir," grinned his sergeant. "It was a bit different from my assignment to the Afghan border."

"I'll bet," said Hartley, whose estimation of his sergeant had risen tremendously after his undercover work abroad. Hartley himself had worked undercover in the Intelligence Corps along the East German frontier during the Cold War when he was doing his National Service. "And you didn't need any managerial skills or pre-operational method working undercover or on the beat," he continued, searching through the mass of papers on his desk.

Unlike Sgt Khan, Hartley was lacking in managerial skills. His desk was littered with notes and the bookshelves behind his chair were an untidy mixture of criminal law, theology and English literature classics.

Already he'd been carpeted by Donaldson, who liked the whole station to be as prissy as his own office. The telling-off had had no effect. Managerial skills were not Hartley's forte, and in the end his boss gave up on him.

Inspector Hartley met Robin Wilkins again when the latter called in at the police station to renew his shot-gun licence, as he was hosting some business friends staying in Ilkesworth during the grouse-shooting season. Hartley happened to be in the reception office and was greeted by the banker.

"Ah, Inspector Hartley! How good to see you. I trust you're keeping well?" he said effusively, shaking the inspector's hand warmly.

"I'm keeping busy," Hartley replied, then said, "There's always rum folk in Keighworth doing rum business like everywhere else. It's not always the backwater place it seems."

The irony was not lost on Wilkins but he masked his reaction with bluff. "No place is free of crime," he replied, then said piously, "it's part of human nature. As a priest you'll be well aware of that eh?"

"I would hope so, sir," said Hartley. "I've been in the job long enough."

With a hint of cynicism, the other asked Hartley how he reconciled his vocation as a priest with his profession of policeman.

"Both fight against evil in the world, sir," said Hartley, rather surprised by the turn of direction in their conversation. However, further discussion was halted when Donaldson appeared and began truckling up to Wilkins, the new big-name on his list.

Wilkins explained he'd popped in to renew his shot-gun licence. "I'm hosting some business contacts over at Ilkesworth for a spot of grouse-shooting," he explained. "Perhaps you'd like to join us one evening for drinks, Arthur. You, too, Hartley if you're free," he added, turning to the inspector. The invitation had a motive. He wanted to find out how far Hartley had got with the investigations about his wife's death at Utworth.

Superintendent Donaldson jumped at the invitation. He lived in Ilkesworth and would revel in the company of Wilkins and his big-wigs. Hartley was about to refuse but had second thoughts. Just as Wilkins wanted to know more about him, he was keen to learn more about Wilkins and what he was up to, so he accepted the invitation. But he'd no stomach for grouse-shooting or any blood-sports. Nonetheless, he duly turned up at the Moorside Hotel and mingled with the well-heeled grouse-killers.

The Moorside Hotel stood solid on the hillside just below the moors. It was a huge place and dominated the vista across the valley to the town and the hills the other side. Ilkesworth was a spa town with an elite resident population, which was why Arthur and Phoebe Donaldson had gone to live there from Keighworth. Of course Arthur revelled in the company that Wilkins was hosting that evening at the Moorside Hotel. He met an old boy from his school in Axminster and two from his college in Cambridge, so he was in his element.

Hartley less so. He'd been brought up in a working class street in Keighworth, had gone to the local grammar school on a scholarship, and had then done his National Service after leaving his sixth-form at the age of eighteen. After a two-year stint in the army he entered police college before going on the beat in a tough area of London. When the chance came he returned north to his beloved Keighworth, first as sergeant then promotion to inspector. Standing by himself that night in the hotel, he was cornered by Wilkins who desperately wanted to know where investigations were going into his wife's death.

He was full of bonhomie as he greeted the inspector, nodding across to the noisy crowd Donaldson was with. "Your boss is in fine form tonight," he began.

"Aye," said Hartley. "He's a good talker. Especially when he's had a drink or two."

"And I hope you're enjoying yourself, Hartley," said the other.

"With a glass of Glenfiddich whisky in my hand, I can enjoy myself anywhere," said Hartley. Wilkins laughed but the smile left his face when Hartley went on, "Oh, by the way, sorry to talk shop, but when I made enquiries at your home in Utworth, on the day Mrs Wilkins died, a Renault car was seen in the drive. It had French number plates, but had gone by the time I arrived. Any idea who might have owned it, sir?"

Wilkins thought for a moment, then said, "Ah, yes. That would be the courier from my office in Paris. He'd be delivering urgent confidential correspondence for me to deal with when I went home for the weekend with my wife...my late wife," he added looking sad. But he wasn't grief-stricken as Hartley would have expected a recently bereaved husband to be. Wilkins showed no sign of being heart-broken.

"I collected my correspondence when I arrived home that terrible day Lucinda took her life. She seemed so contented the last time I saw her," he said, followed quickly by, "Have you made any progress investigating her death? You said there was some doubt about its being suicide. If it wasn't suicide it could only have been murder."

By now the smile had left his face. He looked worried as he awaited

Hartley's reply.

"We haven't ruled out suicide, sir, but I can't comment further," said Hartley doggedly.

Wilkins looked irritated but merely said, "Of course. I quite understand." Then he switched the conversation to grouse-shooting and what a fine day's sport they'd had. It wasn't sport in Hartley's book, but he sipped his whisky and listened politely, putting in the odd word now and then, but mainly listening to Wilkins. The more he talked, the more the inspector learned about him.

During the course of the evening, Wilkins invited Donaldson to a round of golf at Utworth golf club, where he'd been a member for years. He said he was also inviting the Chief Commissioner for the Metropolitan Police, who was one of his shooting-party. Donaldson was flattered beyond measure and went up a score of notches in his own estimation. Here was an opportunity to cosy up to the top man in the London police. If he played his cards right he could accelerate his return to the South. He also now had another name on his name-drop list.

When asked by Wilkins to bring along a partner for their round of golf, Donaldson said he had a top-ranking golfer at Keighworth police station: Sgt Khan with his Oxford Blue.

"Just the ticket!" beamed Wilkins. "He'll ratchet up the standard of play." And little did he know what else Sgt Khan been ratcheting up under cover on Wilkins' patch in Pakistan. And so, one fine sunny morning the foursome met at Utworth golf club for a round of golf, where a very garrulous Donaldson talked them round the course.

The clubhouse had been part of an old hill farm until Utworth had expanded as a rich suburb of the town and the farm and the land had been transformed into the golf club. The farmhouse itself had been extensively renovated. A comfortable bar had been added, along with members' changing rooms and showers.

Above the Utworth course was another, newer, golf club, the Ruddledene club, perched on the hillside beyond a canal, along which leisure barges plied now that commercial traffic had ceased. Higher still were the moors which surrounded the town and straddled the length of the Pennine hills.

Donaldson wangled it so that he partnered the Commissioner and could chat him up all afternoon. Sgt Khan partnered Wilkins, who rambled on unwittingly about his investment in Jalalabad. "To promote industrial growth in the region," he explained patronisingly. He knew that Khan's family came from Karachi and he asked if Khan had ever visited the port.

"I've stayed there with relatives once or twice," Khan replied guardedly. He asked if Wilkins went there often, as he'd said he had an office there.

"I look in now and again. I have an office and warehouse in Karachi from which the mills at Jalalabad I'm investing in are serviced," said Wilkins. "By the way, one of my Karachi drivers comes from Bradford. He's a first-class fellow called Abdul Quereshi. Know him?"

Sgt Khan smiled quietly to himself and said they'd grown up together in the same district of the city. They'd gone to the same primary school. But he said nothing about Quereshi's shady past and present and was relieved that Quereshi had said nothing about his escort on the Jalalabad runs.

By the time they reached the sixteenth hole, Wilkins had told the sergeant much about himself and his investments. He hoped to invest more in Keighworth and had already bought property there. Then, as with Hartley, he asked Khan how enquiries were going about his wife's suicide.

Khan was non-committal. He was sorry to hear of Mrs Wilkins' death. It must have come as a great shock. Wilkins didn't reply at once. He said nothing till he'd played the shot he was concentrating on. Then he glossed over her death with, "In banking one has to take this sort of thing in one's stride. Emotion can ruin business. One has to remain calm and impassive."

Then they made their way back to the clubhouse. But the more Khan got to know the man, the less he liked him. His whole focus in life was making money and below his veneer of bonhomie and polish, there was something evil.

## CHAPTER NINE

Superintendent Donaldson sat in his office wringing his hands yet again. Another murder had been committed in Keighworth and he was beginning to regret his new appointment. Managerial organisation and traffic control were his forte; not homicide. And now he was landed with another killing in the town; this time at Clymo's garage.

When he met Wilkins the same day, he cosied up to him more than ever, apologising for what had happened at the banker's new venture in town and promising they'd do all they could to find the killer. Inspector Hartley and Sgt Khan were at the murder scene along with the forensic team.

The victim was the smooth-talking salesman whom Hartley had interviewed. He was Philip Jackson, a nephew of the garage owner, Jack Clymo, who'd been a famous racing driver in his younger days. Locally he was renowned for another fast life – with women. He'd been married and divorced twice and currently was running foot-loose. Free with his money, he was never short of friends of both sexes. His fame as a racing driver brought in many wealthy clients who snapped up his expensive cars. So he had a ready investor in Robin Wilkins when he wanted to expand his business. And after the death of his second wife, Wilkins had more capital to invest.

Philip Jackson had been shot in the head at close range. His murder seemed to have been deliberately planned. The killer had walked into the office and, as Jackson stood up to greet him, had pulled out a gun and shot him before calmly turning and walking out of the office. He then climbed into a parked car and drove off at speed before anyone realised what had happened.

"I just can't understand it," Jack Clymo kept saying. "Poor Philip hadn't an enemy in the world. Who'd want to kill him?"

"Who, indeed," said Hartley, stroking his chin and looking thoughtfully at the body. Sgt Khan busied himself at the other end of the room, well away from the corpse. He'd no stomach for dead bodies covered in blood.

"Did anyone take the number-plate of the car the killer drove off in?" asked Hartley.

"No, inspector," he replied. "It all happened so quickly.

Dr Dunwell, the forensic pathologist, who'd been kneeling by the body, stood up. He brushed back the one lock of grey hair straddling his bald head and polished his glasses before saying, "He was killed at close range. The bullet took half his skull away." He pointed to the mess on the floor as his assistants tested the desk and area round it for fingerprints.

Sgt Khan glanced across quickly then wished he hadn't and turned away again. It seemed the back of the corpse's head had been blown away. Meanwhile, Dr Dunwell strolled behind the salesman's desk and with his tweezers pulled a bullet from the wall, placing it carefully in a plastic bag.

"There's the culprit," he said, passing the bag to Hartley. "Let the arms experts examine it. They'll tell you what weapon it came from."

Hartley thanked Dr Dunwell, who packed his bag and left, winking at the whey-faced Khan as he passed. When he'd gone, Hartley and Khan looked round the rest of the garage. All was of the best for no expense had been spared. Wilkins had funded it well.

Behind the showrooms were well-equipped working areas where teams of mechanics attended to the expensive cars brought in for repair. Hartley chatted to one of the mechanics because he was surprised at the number of cars being repaired. He asked where they all came from.

"From all over the country," the workman answered. "This one, " he said, nodding at the vehicle he was working on, "was brought up from London yesterday." It was a BMW and looked new. "But this," he continued pointing at the car next to it," was brought in from Hull." Like the rest it was top-range, an expensive Aston Martin.

Hartley thanked him and wandered round with Khan, looking at the rest of the cars. There must have been millions of pounds lined up in gleaming rows before him. He thanked the mechanic, then he and Khan went back into town for their lunch: Khan to the station canteen but, because it was a fine day, Hartley decided he'd eat his pack of sandwiches in the grounds of Crag Castle.

Mary packed a sandwich lunch every day for Blake to eat wherever he found himself working. There were no messages waiting for him back at his office so he decided to make the most of the fine weather and stroll to the castle and eat his lunch outdoors.

The lunchtime visitors were in the restaurant at the rear of the castle, so Hartley enjoyed a bit of peace and quiet by himself, sitting in front of the impressive building, where he had a splendid view across the grounds to the hillside beyond which climbed to the moors on the horizon.

As he ate his sandwiches, he drank in the peace of the gardens and grounds – an oasis of quiet surrounded by the bustling town. Nearby a thrush was in full voice, joining the chorus of birdsong which drifted through the trees and shrubbery. Across the valley Ruddledene and its golf-course lay gleaming in the sun; higher still was the line of dark moorland rimming a cloudless sky. And as he ate Hartley was a dimension away from the sordid world of crime he had to return to after lunch.

Crag Castle was a mock Scottish baronial edifice built in the nineteenth century by a wealthy manufacturer. It was full of happy memories for Hartley. He used to gaze at the turrets from his boyhood home down Garlic Lane, beckoning him to another world. The castle had become run-down in the twentieth century when the last owner moved down south to an estate there to play the aristo. A self-made Keighworth benefactor then bought it for the town, and it became an educational museum and art gallery, replacing the old museum in Albert Park which became a recreation centre.

Blake Hartley often wandered round the building in his spare time. As well as the happy memories of boyhood, there was always something new on display, painting exhibitions and suchlike. So he was very content on that sunny day, eating his sandwich and looking out on the hillside beyond. Then he had company.

"Good afternoon, inspector," said someone joining him on the park bench. It was Stanley Parker, the chauffeur of Robin Wilkins.

Hartley greeted him and asked after his father, who'd lived down Garlic Lane. After more small-talk the conversation turned to Philip Jackson, the murdered car-salesman.

"Terrible affair that murder at Clymo's garage," said Parker. "Philip Jackson delivered an engine part at my place only last week. Rum business altogether."

Hartley glanced across at him. His tone suggested he wasn't entirely happy as Wilkins' chauffeur and wanted to unburden himself.

"Aye. It's a rum business, as you say. First Mrs Wilkins' death and now this killing. What did you make of Mrs Wilkins' death? You were in the house at the time."

The other didn't answer straightaway but gazed across the gardens thoughtfully. Then he turned to Hartley and said, "It came as a shock, inspector. She appeared quite normal. In fact, just before it all happened she came into the garage and asked if the Rolls would be ready for her to go shopping in Harrogate that afternoon. She was looking forward to it. Then the next thing I knew was that she'd hanged herself. It didn't tie up at all."

Hartley nodded and asked if there'd been any visitors to the house that day.

"None as far as I know," said the other. "But not long after she'd been to ask if the car would be ready for her to go shopping in Harrogate, I heard a car in the drive; but when I went out later there was nothing there."

Parker clearly wanted to talk to someone about that day. He lit up a cigarette after asking if Hartley minded.

"Not at all," said Hartley. He didn't smoke himself but he sensed there was more to come about the Wilkinses.

"I'd a lot to thank Mrs Wilkins for," began Parker. "She was generous and gave me a good start in life. Before I became her chauffeur I'd been working for next to nothing as a garage hand ever since I left school at fourteen. I thought I was stuck there for life till the job was advertised for a second chauffeur for Lady Lucinda Haggas, as she then was. Her first husband was Sir Frederick Haggas, who owned Haggas Engineering, one of the biggest textile engineering works in the north."

"I remember him," said Hartley. "So when he died she must have been worth a pound or two."

"Millions. She inherited millions and that's why Wilkins married her. He was much younger than her and needed some ready capital – but this is all in confidence, inspector," he added quickly.

"Of course," Hartley replied. His hunch had been right. Young Parker clearly wanted to unburden himself to someone he could trust. He'd no one else he could speak to in confidence about the past.

Parker took a few more pulls at his cigarette then said quietly, "You know, Wilkins isn't all he seems. He's all charm and hair-oil to his clients and the like; but he treats me like dirt. He'd have sacked me years ago but for his wife. She was very loyal and kind to me. He'd give me the push right now but I know too much."

"In what way?" asked Hartley.

"He conned Lady Haggas all right," said the chauffeur. "He was much younger, and he smooth-tongued her into wedlock after she'd fallen for him. You know what women are like, inspector."

"Some of 'em," said Hartley. His own marriage had been one of mutual love between himself and Mary.

"Anyway," went on the chauffeur, "after inheriting all his first wife's money, too, he was able to forge ahead with his bank. He's dabbled in all sorts of deals since – some of them very shady. I've driven him to downtown places to meet clients I wouldn't trust a penny with. I know some of them had done time – as crooked as a pig's tail."

"Perhaps that's what big banking is all about. As long as the profits flow in, you don't ask where they're coming from. Some bankers don't know right from wrong; and they're supposed to be the pillars of society," said Hartley.

"It's strange how both his wives died so quickly: one in the swimming pool and the other found hanging from the banister," said Parker.

"Very strange," observed Hartley. "The coroner left an open verdict on the first wife. The maid said Mrs Wilkins had had a visitor while she was bathing, but they never discovered who he was. Someone with a foreign accent the maid said. He left just before the body was found."

"And the second Mrs Wilkins also had an unknown visitor just before she was found. Coincidence?" asked Parker, looking across at Hartley for an answer.

"I wonder," Hartley replied, thoughtfully stroking his chin. Events were beginning to unfold at last.

## CHAPTER TEN

When Hartley turned up for work the next day there was an urgent message asking him to see Dr Dunwell at the pathology lab. He took Sgt Khan with him thinking it would give him more experience. It did – but not in the way his boss imagined.

Poor Khan had no stomach for mangled bits of bodies in formalin. The pathologist's office was littered with samples, bottled products of homicide used in lectures which he gave to students from the medical school and police trainees.

One ghastly exhibit especially sickened Khan; the head of a murder victim who'd been axed. His face stared in horror from its glassy grave. One eyelid had dropped while the other stared out in shock. Khan was at once repelled yet fascinated by the thing; drawn to look at it as he entered the room before switching his gaze firmly out of the window. How Khan detested those pathology lab visits his boss made him attend, supposedly for his own good.

After greeting them, Gus Dunwell poured them a cup of tea then turned to a file on his desk. "I've completed the post-mortem on Mrs Wilkins," he began, "and your suspicion was right, Blake. It wasn't suicide. It was murder. She died from drowning. From the marks on her throat, I'd say the killer gripped her round the neck then held her head under water, probably in the bathroom, till she died. Then her body was strung up from the banister to look like suicide."

"Any clues left by the killer?" asked Hartley.

"Not a thing. It was a professional job. I'm going to look again through the first Mrs Wilkins' file to see if there are any similarities as both were drowned. It was assumed that Sandra Wilkins had blacked out while she was having a swim in the pool where they found her."

"And if I remember aright, a stranger also called at the house that day as happened with the second Mrs Wilkins. Wasn't that so, Khan?" he said, turning to his sergeant.

Sgt Khan stopped looking through the window and said his boss was correct. It was Khan who'd interviewed the maid the day her mistress had died.

"So it looks as if we may have a professional killer to deal with," said Dunwell.

"A professional who knew exactly what he was doing in both murders. The question now is whether or not our mutual friend Mr Robin Wilkins knew the killer," said Hartley.

"The ball's in your court, Blake. I've done my bit of sleuthing," said Gus Dunwell, wishing them good-day as they left his lab.

By sheer coincidence, when the two detectives arrived back at the police station, Wilkins was there, renewing his shot-gun licence and hob-nobbing with Superintendent Donaldson in his office. It irked Donaldson when his inspector and sergeant came back, for Wilkins cut short his conversation with him and turned at once to Hartley who'd been summoned to his boss's office.

Generally, Donaldson kept him standing but this time he invited him to sit down. "Mr Wilkins was asking me how the enquiries are going into his late wife's death," began Donaldson. " Perhaps you could up-date him yourself, Hartley, as you're the investigating officer."

"Oh, things are progressing, Mr Wilkins," Hartley answered casually. "But they aren't as straightforward as we thought at first."

"Oh?" said the other, and there was no mistaking the alarm in his voice. Donaldson shuffled uncomfortably in his chair. He didn't want Wilkins dropping off his list so soon.

"Was your wife expecting a visitor on the day she died" asked Hartley.

Wilkins frowned. "I really couldn't say," he replied. "I was in London at the time. We ran our lives separately when I was in Town. Why do you ask, inspector?"

"I believe she was murdered," said Hartley bluntly. "In fact, I think both your wives died the same way – by drowning.

"Good God!" exclaimed Wilkins, but his reaction was hollow. Hartley went on to say what the pathologist had discovered. Wilkins became clearly agitated and took his leave fairly promptly.

Meanwhile, Donaldson stood by, scarcely believing what he'd heard, for Hartley, of course, had been unable to update him. When Wilkins had gone, Donaldson complained he'd been embarrassed by what Hartley had said. His inspector had clearly upset Robin Wilkins.

"I'm sorry, sir," Hartley replied, "but I only found out the facts myself from Dr Dunwell this morning. The two wives had been drowned and a stranger had visited the house shortly before their bodies were discovered."

"Any idea who he was?" asked Donaldson.

"Not yet, sir, but we're working on it," said Hartley, who'd learned much more about Mrs Wilkins from her husband's behaviour in the superintendent's office that day; so had Arthur Donaldson.

Before they parted he asked Hartley to keep him updated about the deaths of the two women. He didn't want to be caught on the hop again with Wilkins or anybody else whose name he dropped regularly in company.

The next day Hartley decided to visit the Mayfair restaurant, the posh place over the shopping arcade where Keighworth's smart set met for morning coffee and daily tittle-tattle. Although it had changed its name since the days when rogue lawyer Simon Grimstone had frequented it daily for his coffee break and lunch, whilst also keeping abreast of goings-on in Keighworth, it was still at the core of the town's gossip. Hartley sat in Grimstone's old look-out spot, an alcove by the window, from where he could observe discreetly the comings and goings of clients in the restaurant and peer through the net curtain to watch the townsfolk in the main street without showing his face.

Hartley sipped his coffee alone, pondering on Harry Hung Wo's tip-off about drug-pushing at the restaurant. From what Khan had said, he knew the source of the heroin that was circulating around Bradford and the nearby towns. What he wanted to know now was who was pushing the drugs among Keighworth's elite. He didn't have to wait long to find out.

A few minutes after Hartley arrived, Feisal Quereshi, a brother of Abdul, came in accompanied by a well-dressed stranger. Feisal was a partner in the family firm of estate agents at Skipworth, which had acted for Robin Wilkins when he bought property in the area. But it proved obvious that Wilkins was also making use of them as a go-between for selling the heroin he was importing from Karachi.

The pair occupied a table in a corner and were served their coffee before being joined shortly afterwards by a fashionably dressed and heavily made-up young woman, who began speaking earnestly with them. Hartley saw them haggling about something; then the woman opened a voluminous shopping bag and passed them what looked like a large wad of fifty pound notes. Hartley watched them closely.

When Quereshi had counted the money, his accomplice slid out some white plastic packets from his attaché case which the woman quickly put into her shopping bag. Then the accomplice peeled off some of the notes Quereshi had handed him and gave them back. That done, they all drained their coffee cups and left. Hung Wo's tip-off was right. The restaurant was being used by drug-pushers.

As the trio left, two women came in to the restaurant, both of them well-known to Hartley: his boss's wife, Daphne Donaldson, and her friend, Doris Kettlewell, the Lady Mayoress of Keighworth, whose husband was also a mason. Daphne spoke with a loud home-counties accent which her friend tried to imitate but failed. Her northern up-bringing was too ingrained.

Both Doris and Daphne were expensively dressed, for they shopped in London on regular visits to the capital. They met each day at the Mayfair restaurant with other friends for morning coffee and a gossip, looking round the room to see who else was there. Hartley was caught by Daphne's eagle eye as he tried to leave surreptitiously.

"Inspector Hartley," she barked across the room. "Fancy seeing you here! Do you come regularly?"

Hartley paused then went to greet her. "Good morning, Mrs Donaldson," he said, pulling a smile onto his face. And nodding at the Lady Mayoress. "No I don't come here often, but I'd heard they make a good cup of coffee."

Daphne gave her flashlight smile and said, "Of course, you'll have met Mrs Kettlewell, the Lady Mayoress, in the course of duty."

"Indeed," said the inspector. "I've had the pleasure of keeping a watchful eye on her and the Mayor on various occasions."

Doris Kettlewell smiled approvingly and as a parting comment Daphne added, "It's so pleasant meeting up and having coffee at a place like this in town. Quite special, eh? Good service and the right clientèle. So many restaurants have the wrong sorts frequenting them in Keighworth; drug-pushers and the like. At least here you know you're dining in decent company."

Hartley smiled again – and this time he didn't force his smile. He only wished the ladies good-day and left.

## CHAPTER ELEVEN

Ibrahim Khan had three cousins in Karachi who were high-ranking policemen. They were experienced officers working under very difficult conditions for Karachi was a violent place. Not only were there rival gangs slugging it out, holding onto their own patches, but there were areas where Pathan refugees had settled, and others where the Taliban were in control; and all of them waged war against the police, who valiantly tried to keep some semblance of law and order.

Over the years many policemen had been killed and their leaders were constantly targeted. One of Khan's cousins, Inspector Hussein Khan, had been badly wounded in a shoot-out, but he'd pulled through and was determined to enforce law in the city. He stayed with the Khans in Britain when he flew in to make enquiries about a luxury car, a Rolls Royce, belonging to a Taliban chief, which the Karachi police had seized.

When forensics had dismantled part of it, they discovered that the serial numbers on the chassis didn't correspond with those on other parts of the car. The car was probably stolen and had been tampered with. After prolonged questioning of its Taliban owner, they discovered he'd received it as a sweetener from the managing director of the textile company at Jalalabad which Wilkins was financing.

Inspector Hussein Khan wanted his cousin Ibrahim to find out more, and after some discreet enquiries, Sgt Khan discovered that the car had come from Clymo's garage. He also found out there was a regular supply of luxury cars going from the garage via Hull to Wilkins' warehouses in Karachi.

Inspector Hartley knew at once who to see. He and Khan interviewed Stanley Parker, the disaffected chauffeur at Fairfield House. They knew he didn't get on with his boss and through Parker they had a lead into Clymo's garage for he went there regularly to have his Rolls Royce serviced and knew the mechanics well.

The detectives found out in the course of their investigations that two of the mechanics had done time in prison not long before. They'd been jailed for stealing cars then selling them on after changing their number plates and re-spraying them. Forging registration papers was a simple matter, then in the second-hand market there was a ready trade. Parker was to tell them more in due course.

One day, while he was waiting for his Rolls to be serviced, Parker saw a damaged Mercedes brought into the garage on the back of a trailer. To kill time, he chatted with the garage hand who'd brought in the damaged car. "It'll cost a bomb to whoever owns that having it put right," he commented, nodding at the damaged Mercedes.

"We'll cannibalise it – use it for spare parts," the mechanic replied.

"So, what do you do with the repaired cars then?" asked Parker.

The other grinned, then lowered his voice. "The boss has contacts abroad we sell 'em to. Mr Clymo's well-known in the car-trade. He built up a good reputation as a racing driver and does a deal of business here and abroad with luxury cars."

Parker changed the subject and mentioned it was a nasty business Philip Jackson being murdered. Had they any idea yet who killed him? The other didn't answer at once but kept his head down working on the damaged car. Moments later, as he wiped the oil from his hands, he said, "They say it was summat to do wi' a London gang who didn't like their patch being poached."

"Poached?" echoed Parker.

"Aye – nicking cars from their part of London," said the mechanic, who then clammed up.

However, Parker did more probing as he strolled round the garage waiting for his car, chatting to the garage hands. He discovered that Jack Clymo drove to London regularly with a co-driver – then returned with two cars; one of which was stolen and very expensive. Those London trips were professional operations which targeted only the best.

But he targeted one too many when he nicked a gang-leader's car off his own patch. Poor Jackson, Clymo's co-driver, was recognised and paid the price of driving the stolen car back to Keighworth. The gang-leader sent a hit-man up north to square accounts.

"Well, "said Hartley after Parker told him all this, "that's cleared up one mystery. We now know why Philip Jackson was killed. Now we have to find out who did it, and that will involve the metropolitan police. They have their tabs on the London gangs. Our Mr Robin Wilkins has his sticky little fingers in more murky pies than merchant banking, it seems."

The Quereshis weren't in the same league as the London criminals, but at times they were drawn into their orbit. Once you're into the criminal underworld, it's difficult to get out of it, as Abdul Quereshi found out when he was leaned on to ferry yet another consignment of textile equipment to Jalalabad – plus the hidden arms for the Taliban.

Though he tried hard, he couldn't wriggle out when Wilkins virtually ordered him to drive there again. Quereshi knew that if he refused there'd be reprisals. Wilkins wasn't a man to lock horns with. And he paid well. But Quereshi knew he might have to pay with his life if he accepted the job. So again he scurried to Ibrahim Khan for help.

Special Branch had known about Wilkins and his connection with the Taliban for some time and were keeping their tabs on him. Sgt Khan was transferred again to work for them, ostensibly visiting family in Karachi.

He assumed the name of Jangeer Ali again and flew out to Karachi with his cousin, Inspector Hussein Khan. When they arrived, he was surprised to see two guards outside his cousin's house and Inspector Khan explained why. Two years earlier he'd been targeted by the Taliban and badly wounded, but courageously he'd gone back to duty, determined, like his fellow officers, to fight the Taliban and other criminals in the city.

After a brief stop in Karachi, Inspector Khan joined Quereshi and Ibrahim Khan in the lorry they were driving to Jalalabad, travelling in the back with an automatic rifle. They set off for the border in the morning but immediately ran into trouble. Just outside Karachi four gunmen on motorcycles drew alongside the lorry and ordered them to stop.

"Drive on!" shouted Hussein from the back of the lorry, and Quereshi put his foot down; but as they sped past, the gunmen opened fire, tailing the lorry as it raced along the highway. They were about to overtake it and fire at the cab when Hussein opened fire with his rifle, bowling them over like ninepins Their bikes skidded over and the gunmen fell off, lying wounded by their bikes in the road.

"Don't stop! Keep driving!" yelled Hussein from the back of the lorry. "The local police will deal with them!"

It was to be the first of several incidents along the border road to Jalalabad. At one point, high in the mountains above Quetta, they were held up by local tribesmen who were at odds with the Taliban. Ibrahim Khan managed to contact the textile mills and in a short time a contingent of Taliban fighters appeared.

After a brief exchange of fire, the tribesmen fled. For the rest of the way, the Khans and Quereshi were escorted by the Taliban. The irony of the situation wasn't lost on the Khans. They joked about it afterwards;

how the cross-border criminals they were fighting in Karachi guarded them to their destination in a lorry driven by a petty criminal from Bradford.

A surprise awaited their arrival in Jalalabad. Wilkins had flown in by private jet on the nearby air-strip to see how things were going at the textile plant. His unexpected presence caught Sgt Khan on the hop; he surreptitiously left the cab and found a hiding place nearby. His cousin Hussein slipped into the co-driver's seat and was able to listen in while Quereshi did all the talking with Wilkins. The inspector learned much from the conversation, especially how the Taliban were being armed and how heroin grown in the region was being transported back to Karachi and beyond.

Robin Wilkins in Pakistan was a very different person from the smooth-talking merchant banker who buttered up folk like the Donaldsons in Keighworth. He was now a hard-faced crook dealing with his own kind, haggling with Taliban leaders about arms deals and heroin, and buying stocks of heroin to sell in Europe.

"Who's your co-driver?" he asked Quereshi, looking suspiciously at Hussein Khan.

"A friend from Bradford," Quereshi replied.

Inspector Khan grinned and said "We're cousins three times removed and we both speak local Karachi Urdu."

Wilkins seemed satisfied with his answer and laughed, quipping, "And the more you're removed from him the better if the police get onto him."

Quereshi gave a hollow laugh, too, but his boss was nearer the truth than he thought. Wilkins then went to supervise the unloading of the lorry, making sure that heroin went into the sealed place which the Taliban took their weapons from.

The whole operation in a secluded part of the textile plant took only half an hour. Once they had their weapons and ammunition, the Taliban melted back into the hills. Satisfied his heroin was safely on board and sealed in, Wilkins looked over the new mills to see how they were faring, making sure his investment was holding up.

It was a large textile plant built to employ over a thousand men. Mill chimneys sprouted everywhere, fired with coal and belching smoke. Half the plant contained cotton looms and the other half woollen looms. The cloth they produced had a ready market in Karachi and other cities.

Escorted by armed guards, it took Wilkins the better part of the day to look round the plant. Also with him were the mill managers and directors, grovelling to their paymaster. Although surrounded by Taliban and lawless tribesmen, they knew they were safe. Wilkins' wealth was their safeguard. So was his team of ruthless bodyguards.

Yet beneath all that vaunting of wealth and power, there lurked a calculating criminal mind, and a killer prepared to get what he wanted at any cost.

At the end of his tour he returned to his private jet, well satisfied by what he'd seen. He flew back to his suite in Karachi a happy man, but he wouldn't have been so pleased with himself had he known who was on board that lorry with Abdul Quereshi. Inspector Hussein Khan had gathered much useful information, which the Karachi police would act on in the future. Valuable evidence had also been gathered for Special Branch to prosecute Wilkins on his return to Britain.

## CHAPTER TWELVE

Meanwhile, in Keighworth, Blake Hartley was pursuing another line of enquiry. Someone had been stealing charity boxes from the counters of shops and pubs. He suspected it was some wino or junkie stealing for a quick fix, so he paid a regular visit to the parish church graveyard, where a huddle of homeless addicts lived in good weather. When it turned wet or cold, they made for church porches or derelict buildings.

It was a mild day and he enjoyed his walk through the town, wishing acquaintants good-day and feeling very much a part of the old town. As a young copper early in his career on the beat in London, he'd been lonely and yearned for the North – as much as his new boss, Superintendent Donaldson, yearned to go back to the Home Counties and the balmy South.

He'd returned to Keighworth as a sergeant, married and settled into a comfortable middle-age there. Now, an inspector and non-stipendiary Anglican priest, he was fulfilled and very much part of the local scene.

He went regularly to the graveyard group. They were a sad bunch of outcasts and he was sorry for them. "We're all vulnerable to temptations of one sort or another; we all have chinks in our armour. There but for the grace of God go I," came constantly to his mind during his ministry as a policeman/priest – even when he was arresting a wrong-doer.

Mainly Victorian, the graveyard was a large one. The industries and disease over the years in the town had taken their toll. The place was packed; gravestones lying right next to each other, many of them table-gravestones. It was under the largest of these that the Keighworth 'Wine Club' gathered and spent the day swigging bottles of cheap wine or giving themselves a fix.

They didn't live long; few reached forty. They came from all backgrounds and were a sorry lot like the lepers of old; dirty, ill-clad and unwanted. Only when they became very ill or nearing the end of life were they taken into care, usually in an emergency ambulance. More often they were found dead in some derelict building surrounded by empty liquor bottles and rats.

There were half a dozen of them anchored to the large table-grave of Aaron Butterfield, a Victorian mill-owner, who'd passed away on 12 September 1888. Three winos sat on the ornate gravestone glugging their poison, though it was only ten o'clock in the morning.

"Morning, Sam," said Hartley to their leader, and nodded to the others. "How's things?"

Sam Duxworth was the oldest of the bunch, and after a swig at his bottle he returned the inspector's greeting, holding up his bottle. "Fine, boss. Just fine now I've had me medicine," he said.

Hartley glanced over the bunch for newcomers, but he recognised them all. From time to time, strangers drifted into the town and joined them, but the group on the gravestone that day were homebred drop-outs. A couple were from families that he knew and his heart went out to their parents. He was himself a family man and knew what they'd be going through.

"Owt fresh, Sam?" asked Hartley.

"Most days are the same. How about you, boss?" asked the other.

Hartley came straight to the point. "There's somebody nicking charity boxes from the shops and pubs. You don't by any chance know who, do you?"

Sam didn't reply. He took another swig of wine, but the junkie sitting next to him said, "There were that chap who came 'ere last week. The one who talked posh an' looked so poorly. The one who were counting the cash from an Oxfam box. You remember?"

"I remember 'im now," said Duxworth, wiping his mouth. "He were a loner. Kept 'imself to 'imself. He said he were kipping in them houses they're demolishing down Beck Street behind t'market. I haven't seen 'im about since though. He weren't really one of us."

"Did you get his name?" asked Hartley.

"No, boss. Like I said he just turned up here cadging a drink 'cos he were skint – that is, till he came back with that Oxfam box. He chucked it away when he'd emptied it," said Duxworth.

Hartley asked where the box had been discarded, and found it under an adjoining table-grave. He put it into a plastic bag for the forensic department to examine later; then he re-joined the group. As was his custom he led them to a nearby fish-and-chip shop, strung out behind him like a latter day Pied Piper. There, he treated them to the only decent meal they'd eat that day.

He left them tucking into their meal and walked to Beck Street, where they were demolishing a row of old terrace houses to build a new apartment block. The houses being demolished were slum properties where the homeless kipped.

The end house in the terrace had obviously been used recently because the door had been forced. Hartley pushed it open with his foot and called out, "Is anyone in there?" There was no reply so he went in, treading carefully over the rotten wooden floors.

Someone had recently been kipping there. There was ash in the fireplace, and a decrepit old sofa nearby. There was also a pile of wood from broken chairs and doors. As Hartley trod gingerly through the place the odd rat scurried away. In a back room he found what he was looking for – a heap of discarded charity boxes among other litter.

He mounted the rotten staircase gingerly after calling out again. The doors were missing off all the bedrooms, and in the second one he saw two of the doors nailed crudely together to form a makeshift sleeping cubby-hole which kept whoever was kipping there free from draughts.

He peered into it and saw a body huddled under a dirty blanket lying on a soiled mattress; the body of a man who'd been dead some time from the stench. His swollen face had been chewed by rats; and by the body was an empty wine bottle and a plastic bag with white powder in it – heroin.

Hartley leaned over the makeshift cubby-hole to look closer. A rat shot out from behind the dead man and disappeared into a hole in the skirting board. The inspector then climbed over the broken doors and searched inside the dead man's coat. He pulled out a wallet and a benefit card on which was the dead man's name, Raymond Arthur Kettlewell. He glanced at the address, then looked harder. It was the address of the Mayor and Mayoress of Keighworth.

When Blake Hartley went to break the news that their son was dead, it all came out. They were shocked and the Revd Det. Insp. Hartley prayed silently for them as they sat together tightly holding hands. They were good honest hard-working folk and had sacrificed much for their only son, sending him to a boarding school and then college before he dropped out high on drugs.

"There'll have to be a formal identification," said Hartley gently.

"I understand," said Rex Kettlewell, choked up.

"Perhaps Mrs Kettlewell might prefer not to go," suggested Hartley. "It won't be a pleasant sight."

The mayoress looked up and said firmly through her tears. "I'll go. He's my only child." And the inspector's heart went out to her. He also had a grown-up son and daughter.

Then she poured out the sad story of their son. "We gave him everything," she began. "A good home and a good start in life. Perhaps we gave him too much. He never lacked for anything. We loved him dearly."

Hartley nodded sympathetically. "We can only do our best as parents," he offered.

His wife was too overcome by her son's death to say anything for some time, but her husband, Rex, wanted to talk about him. "We sent him to a good school before he went up to Cambridge, and that's where it all went haywire. He got in with the wrong sort and began taking drugs; cannabis at first but then harder stuff. They took over his life and he dropped out of college and fell in with the London drug scene. He came back to Keighworth about a month ago. He got beaten up in London for some reason so it wasn't safe for him to stay there. We thought we might help him go straight when he returned home, but it didn't work out. He wanted to live life his way." He paused before adding almost in a whisper, "You saw what happened, inspector. We're grateful for all your help."

Hartley said he'd take them to the mortuary, and before they left he said a short prayer. Then he drove with them for the identification, before reporting to his boss.

Donaldson was doubly shocked, for Raymond Kettlewell had been an undergraduate at his old Cambridge college. He naively thought the students there were above taking drugs. It never went on while he was there – but then he came from a different generation.

"Drugs are everywhere, sir," Hartley said. "They run through society from top to bottom like a cancer."

Donaldson looked up at the college rowing oar with his name on it on the wall behind his desk. "You and I have lived in a different world from the present generation, Hartley." he said. "I must confess that what youngsters get up to these days is quite beyond me."

On that subject they both agreed. The problem would come when the press got hold of young Kettlewell's death. How were the police going to cushion the leading citizens of Keighworth from the inevitable furore which would follow? Donaldson hummed and aahed for a moment, then said, "As superintendent I'd deal with the press myself; but as a man of the cloth you might be more suitable."

And so it transpired. It was Hartley who briefed the press at the police station the next day about the body found in the derelict house. It was Hartley, too, who took the funeral. Daphne Donaldson's visits to the Mayfair restaurant with Doris Kettlewell became fewer, and in time stopped altogether when Doris's term as mayoress ended.

## CHAPTER THIRTEEN

The death of young Raymond Kettlewell intensified the area drug squad's efforts to clamp down on the flow of heroin into Keighworth. They sent a team from Bradford to liaise with the police in Keighworth where the new superintendent was frantically trying to cope with the spate of homicide and drug-peddling with had hit the town.

The flood of heroin came from Wilkins' deals with the Taliban and the poppy-growers of Afghanistan. Local pushers suddenly had their noses put out of joint when London gangs supplied by Wilkins began supplying cheap heroin in the North.

Wilkins' wealth flourished as the profits from his Jalalabad investment began to roll in. He bought another expensive property in the Yorkshire Dales –an eighteenth century manor house in an estate of eight hundred acres. It cost him a few million but boosted his ego and prestige. The Donaldsons were especially impressed when they were invited to the house-warming party where Wilkins played the country squire.

However, Wilkins retained the house in Utworth for a while, and the housekeeper and chauffeur were left in charge. He employed another chauffeur for his new mansion in the Dales, for he'd never taken to Stanley Parker, his dead wife's driver. He left him and the housekeeper to oversee Fairfield House while he went to live in Grassingley Manor whenever he was in England.

It was at Fairfield House that Stanley Parker made a breakthrough in the inquiry into the deaths of Wilkins' two wives. One day, he was clearing out the garages and came across some old footage from the security cameras round the house. He decided to play them back and among them were images of the days the two Mrs Wilkins had been found dead. On the days they died the same expensive Renault car with French number-plates was parked just inside the entrance. The driver was caught on camera getting out of the car, then returning to it later.

He was tall, dark-haired and well-built with a lean Gallic face. His coat collar was turned up and he wore black gloves and dark glasses. Parker noticed he had a livid scar running down the left side of his face.

The chauffeur passed the footage to Inspector Hartley, who contacted Interpol to check out the car and number-plate. The reply soon came back, for the driver was on Interpol's records. The car was owned by Marcel Lugard, nicknamed Scarface, well known to the French police. He'd done time for armed robbery, and had been involved in notorious gang-fights in Paris. He was currently employed by a dubious security company as a guard at an office block where Wilkins had a suite of offices to operate his merchant bank.

A photo of Scarface was circulated and one of the first to meet him was Superintendent Arthur Donaldson, when he and his wife, Daphne, attended the house-warming party at Grassingley Manor. Robin Wilkins was there to greet his guests with his personal assistant, Cheryl, acting as hostess. He shook hands warmly with the superintendent and gave Daphne two equally warm kisses on both cheeks, which flooded with colour.

"How lovely to see you again," he oozed; then led the couple to a group which included the Chief Constable, Sir William Smith, and the MP for Keighworth, Michael Fletcher. This got the evening off to good start for

Donaldson, who immediately placed the MP on his name-drop list for the following week at work.

"What with homicide and drug-pushing, Keighworth's getting quite a name for itself in the press, Arthur," Sir William said jovially as they shook hands.

Arthur Donaldson put a brave face on it and replied, "Indeed, Sir William. We've been stretched these past few months, especially with the in-flow of heroin."

By this time Wilkins had joined them and caught the tail-end of their conversation. "Heroin dealers have become a real menace in the region where I'm investing in Pakistan, on the Afghan border. There's an enterprising textile group near Jalalabad bringing much needed employment to the region. They're making cloth for sale in Karachi. It's the finest cloth in the country and is being snapped up by shops and tailors in every city. It won't be long before it'll be on sale here – at very competitive prices. I'm expecting a very good return for my investments there," said Wilkins, looking very self-satisfied.

"You were always a pretty canny lot in Keighworth," quipped the Chief Constable.

"You're right, Sir William. You can never pull the wool over a Yorkshireman's eyes especially when they weave it," said Wilkins, winking at Donaldson, who laughed politely; but as a southerner he thought northern humour lacked taste and refinement.

It was when the little group broke up and moved to other parts of the room that the superintendent recognised Scarface from the photo which had been circulated. He looked even more vicious in reality. His swarthy skin highlighted his cold, killer's eyes which moved constantly over those there – almost as if he were selecting his next victim. Donaldson hurried over to Hartley and Khan, guests like himself. He just had to tell his inspector whom he'd seen. However, Hartley had already spotted Scarface, which left his boss deflated.

"I noticed him as soon as I came in, sir," he said coolly. He's Scarface all right. You can't really miss him."

"He looks a nasty piece of work. Bring him in for questioning. The sooner we have him under lock and key, the better," said Donaldson.

"If we move too quickly, sir, he'll go to ground. One step at a time till we're sure we have him. Don't forget, he has a wealthy and powerful employer. Mr Wilkins has a lot of clout. And we've no proof yet that he actually entered Fairfield House on the days the two women were found dead."

"Perhaps you're right, Hartley," said his boss, nibbling his forefinger nervously. "We don't want to queer our pitch. Mr Wilkins moves in high places, as you say."

"And some very low ones, too," thought Hartley to himself.

The evening passed pleasantly enough; but the more Donaldson got to know about his host, the less comfortable he felt. To tell the truth, he was glad Hartley and Khan were there. There were more thugs who were acting as security guards about the place and some of the guests he met made the superintendent cringe. Wilkins certainly mixed with some odd people, yet Donaldson in his innocence simply assumed that was part and parcel of being a merchant banker.

Jack Clymo, the garage owner, was there. Since the murder of his nephew he was more careful where he obtained his cars, and had concentrated on dealing only in the North. London was too dangerous a place to poach in.

Superintendent Donaldson found himself chatting to Clymo during the evening, and as the night wore on he realised he was caught in a web of deceit; and the spider who wove it lurking in the centre was Robin Wilkins.

Of course, Daphne knew nothing of all this. She gushed over Wilkins, who impressed her greatly telling her of all the projects he was investing in. Her husband kept quiet and did his best to get her away, but she clucked on incessantly and kept him in Wilkins' company for much of the evening. At one point, Wilkins enquired about Philip Jackson's murder.

"We're progressing steadily," said Donaldson.

Then Daphne cut in with, "He's got Inspector Hartley and his team on the case."

"Good chap, Hartley," was Wilkins' response. "You lead a fine team at Keighworth."

"Hartley usually gets his man," said Donaldson – at which point Wilkins changed the conversation.

When he managed to get away from Wilkins, Donaldson made a beeline for his inspector and sergeant. They were hidden behind a flower display watching Scarface and his men as they roved around the room.

Scarface's pale eyes were never still, and as he turned his unsmiling face to give orders, the light caught the livid scar which ran down one cheek. The bulge under his left armpit said he was armed. He was a trained killer, having been in the French Foreign Legion. But he'd been drummed out for grave misconduct. His boss, Robin Wilkins, was flying back to Paris the next day and Scarface would be with him.

The evening ended with a spectacular fireworks display which Scarface oversaw, handling the fireworks dexterously. Hartley and Khan watched him closely and collected useful information about him, including a set of fingerprints which was prime evidence later.

## CHAPTER FOURTEEN

When Jack Clymo exported his stolen cars to Karachi, the transporters brought back heroin from Jalalabad. He hid it in his garages and exported it across Europe through a drug-pusher in Holland, ostensibly a market gardener in the Dutch bulb trade. Before he was caught, Clymo made a fortune.

He was uncovered by the Drugs Squad after lengthy covert video surveillance. Following Stanley Parker's discovery of old CCTV footage with Scarface on it, Hartley and Khan looked through the footage from the cameras set up outside Clymo's garage. The cameras clearly revealed Clymo's men unloading heroin on their return from Karachi. Now they had that under their belts, the detectives were ready to pounce and once they had Jack Clymo in the bag, they could go for Wilkins.

Among the old footage found by Parker was a clip of Scarface inside Fairfield House on the day Lucinda Wilkins was found hanged. The clip showed Scarface in the hallway tying his shoelace after he'd taken off his black gloves. Before he put his gloves on, he levered himself up on a cabinet in the hallway.

After they'd seen the clip, Hartley commented, "Let's hope the housekeeper hasn't dusted that cabinet." She hadn't and forensic picked up Scarface's fingerprints. They also found stubs of French cigarettes in the driveway where the Renault car had been parked. The net was tightening and Wilkins was in it.

When an arrest warrant was made for Scarface, Wilkins knew the game was up and flew to Karachi from his Paris office. But when Sgt Khan's cousin and the Karachi police said they wanted to question him, he fled to Jalalabad leaving his guards and office workers to be interrogated by the Karachi police. They also searched his offices and warehouses and gathered enough evidence to arrest him and many of his staff.

Inspector Hussein Khan and his team then flew by helicopter to Jalalabad and were about to land on the air-strip when a hail of bullets hit their craft. They landed behind a small hangar and began exchanging shots with Wilkins' men. Worse was to come.

As they took cover in the hangar, a Taliban fighter fired his rocket-launcher to demolish the helicopter. They were trapped and radioed for help from the army. When an airborne unit arrived a full-scale battle with the Taliban began for control of the textile complex.

The Taliban were well armed and had a plentiful supply of ammunition, but as army reinforcements arrived they became outnumbered and pulled back into the hills. Wilkins went with them and for some time lived rough, moving from hideout to hideout. He knew the game was up but didn't surrender. He'd covert access to bank funds he'd salted away by which he bribed the Taliban to hide him.

He made a reputation for himself as a rogue banker; but his bodyguard, Scarface Marcel Lugard, was killed in a shoot-out with the French police. Some years later, Wilkins himself was killed in a raid by the Karachi police in a luxury village where he had been living secretly.

He'd hoped to live out the rest of his life there under an assumed name, but the gaff was blown by the woman he kept. She became intensely jealous when he began keeping company with a younger woman. Worldly-wise as he was, Wilkins never fathomed the opposite sex. No man does. Had he been more *au fait* with womanhood, he'd have known how a scorned woman feels.

One of his employees who did well out of the whole affair was Stanley Parker, the chauffeur. When Wilkins fled the country, his assets were seized and Parker lost his job. Yet young Parker, enterprising as ever, went on a journalism course at Keighworth College. When he'd completed it, he wrote a best-seller about Wilkins. He detailed how Wilkins got his capital to start merchant banking, by marrying two rich widows then hiring a French hit-man to bump them off. Parker made a mint when his book was published and never looked back.

Inspector Hartley and Sgt Khan featured prominently in the book and came out of it well, which rather piqued their boss, Superintendent Arthur Donaldson, who got no mention. He brought up the topic at the lunch the publishers gave in the Mayfair restaurant (now under new management) to launch the book.

Present were all the local dignitaries including the Chief Constable and Mayor whose company Donaldson and his wife were part of. Daphne made sure of that, for she knew the manageress of the restaurant, who arranged the book-signing and seating of the guests.

Because they featured in the book, Inspector Hartley, Sgt Khan and their wives were also invited to the book-launch; but they were seated at a table well down the pecking–order at the other end of the dining-hall. When he saw them, Donaldson was over in a flash.

"Good to see you here," he began with gusto; then added," Have you read Parker's book? You both get a mention, y'know."

Hartley smiled benignly. "So I see, sir," he replied. "Young Parker kindly sent us signed complimentary copies – not that we really deserved them. After all, we were only doing our duty."

"So was I," said Donaldson. "But I didn't get a mention. As team-leader, I'd have thought he would have said something about me."

Hartley could see his boss was rattled, and although he might have told him exactly why he wasn't mentioned in the book, he thought it more tactful to humour him. After all, it was a happy occasion and they were all dining free at the publishers' expense in the poshest restaurant in Keighworth.

Hartley said placatingly, "It was because you'd just taken up your new post and were so busy settling in, sir. Your arrival coincided with an unusually active period at the station these past few months. In addition to the two murders at Fairfield House you had Wilkins to contend with and all his double-dealing. He conned us all for a time. I don't know how you coped, sir, coming here new in the middle of this spate of crime."

His few words had the desired effect and calmed his boss down. "Anyhow, now we're here we may as well all enjoy ourselves at the publishers' expense, eh?" said Donaldson, who made more small-talk before returning to the top table for the speeches.

A director of the publishing firm made the opening speech outlining the contents and background of the book before Stanley Parker explained how he came to write it.

He said he'd been privileged to play a small part in unmasking a master-criminal; a man who'd conned the British banking system and himself when he was chauffeur. Only by chance had he come across the CCTV footage which enabled Inspector Hartley and his team to uncover the murders at Fairfield House, and put them on the trail of Wilkins, who eventually came to a sticky end in Pakistan.

He concluded "Were it not for the local police force here in Keighworth, Wilkins might still be at large – a veritable Moriarty. One might say it needed a master-copper of Detective Inspector Hartley's stature to catch a master-criminal like Wilkins."

He sat down to loud applause with those present turning to Blake Hartley's table as they applauded – much to Arthur Donaldson's chagrin! But as the lunch wore on, talk of Wilkins drifted to more pleasant topics and a good time was had by one and all – especially the Donaldsons in the company of the Chief Constable and the Keighworth elite.

# Books In The Blake Hartley Series

1. The Bradshaw Mystery

2. The Museum Mystery

3. The Marcham Mystery

4. The Graveyard Mystery

5. The Allotment Mystery

6. Moorland Mystery

7. The Scrap-Yard Mystery

8. The Dance-Hall Mystery

9. The Bandstand Mystery

10. The Merchant Bank Mystery